Brutal Limits
The Lim...

CASTLE VIEW
PRESS

Copyright © 2022 by Marissa Farrar and S R Jones.
All rights reserved.

No portion of this book may be reproduced in any form without written permission from the publisher or author, except as permitted by copyright law.

Cover Photo by FuriousFotog Cover by Marissa Farrar
Edited by Lori Whitwam
Proofread by Jessica Fraser
Published by Castle View Press

If you'd like a super smutty retelling of one of the scenes from the guy's POVs, then grab it here and sign up to Marissa and Skye's newsletters at the same time!
https://BookHip.com/DAGCKZV

Prologue
Wilder
Aged Eight

THE VOICES OF THE CHILDREN soar upward toward the lofty rafters of the church. They sound like angels sending their song to heaven.

I keep my head down, not wanting to look at the man leading the congregation in our weekly worship. I glance to my left where my mother's hand is clutched tightly around the strap of her handbag. Her other hand is held in a firm grip by my stepfather, Robert.

The back of my mother's right hand is drier than the handbag strap. Her skin is lined and cracked like parchment. She's only in her thirties, but her work is hard, she says. Mom spends her days scrubbing and polishing other people's houses.

The rich ladies, those whose houses she cleans, are sitting much farther toward the front of the church than we are. The rich folk always get the best seats because they give the most money. I don't mind that they're sitting way up there. They always stink of too much perfume, and when they try to talk to me, they bend over and put their faces right in mine and talk to me like I'm stupid instead of just being eight.

The song ends, and I glance at the clock on the wall. My heart speeds up. Soon, the service will be over and Sunday school will begin. That means it's time for my private lesson with Pastor Wren.

When I stole the coloring book and sweets from Mr. Jameson's store, I never imagined where it would lead. If I had, I wouldn't have even thought about stealing.

I swing my skinny legs, still too short to hit the floor, and send up a prayer to God. I don't think he listens to me anymore. I think ever since I stole those sweets and the coloring book, God has deserted me. It's the only explanation I can think of as to why life has gotten so difficult.

Pastor Wren begins to speak, and his voice makes my stomach clench in disgust and fear. He talks about love, and respect, and doing one's moral duty—though I don't really understand what that means. He launches into a long, rambling story, something about a donkey and a lion, but I'm not really listening. Instead, in my mind, I'm imagining that this time I will fight back. This time Pastor Wren will be the one to be hurt, not me.

I should tell Mom what is happening to me, but she's already drinking too much again. I heard her talking to her friend, Mandy, on the phone the other day, and it wasn't good things Mom was saying. Her voice was slurred, and her tone bitter. I'd been eavesdropping again, even though Robert says that curiosity killed the cat, so it sure as hell will kill skinny little runts like me.

Mom had told Mandy she can't take much more. She was saying Robert is cruel to her, and he makes life difficult. Then she had added with a bitter laugh, *"But how can I support us without him? The boy eats us out of house and home."* I don't really think I eat any more than most normal kids. It's not as if I'm big. Medium height, but I'm lanky, and weedy.

"Let us now say the Lord's Prayer and then we will take a moment to pray in silent meditation as we reflect upon our sins and ask the Lord for forgiveness. We will also beg him to guide us in the coming week," Pastor Wren says in his scratchy voice.

I learned a new word at school this week. *Hypocrite*. Pastor Wren is a hypocrite. I know that much. I want to stand up in the church and point to him, shouting it at him. I don't do it. I've already caused Mom far too much trouble, what with how I eat us out of house and home, and the stealing, and the getting into trouble at school. Not that the school trouble is my fault. It's the other boys. They bully me.

They laugh at my clothes with the holes in them. Steal my worn shoes after sports and run around hiding them, and they call me *orphan boy*, which makes no sense because I've got a mother. One of them said it was because I reminded him of Oliver. I don't know who Oliver is, and I keep meaning to ask someone, but I don't know who to ask. I could ask Mom, but these days she doesn't have much time for me.

Robert's grip on Mom's hand tightens as the Lord's Prayer ends, and she bows her head further. She almost looks like she is slumping over in her seat, so desperate she is to assume the correct posture for the moment's silent meditation.

"You better pray that you find a way to be a better wife," Robert mutters through clenched teeth.

He keeps his voice low, but it's loud enough for me to hear. I hate him, I think. The thought sends a ripple of fear through my belly. Hate is a sin. Pastor Wren tells us that all the time, and maybe that's why this is happening to me. Because I keep sinning. I think Pastor Wren is a sinner, too, though.

Nearly all the grown-ups I know are either sinners or lost souls.

We learned all about lost souls a few weeks ago, and I think my mama is definitely one of them. Mom isn't a bad person. She is a lost person. Even before she married Robert, she had long bits of time where she'd get so sad. Mom calls them the blues. I don't really know what the blues are. I just know they make Mom drink too much and smoke too much, and not sleep. The days and long weeks when she had the blues, I would walk super quietly around the house so as not to upset her.

I think she might have the blues now, but I think this time they are worse. Maybe this time the blues are darker in color. Maybe this time they are the purples. Not that she'd say anything about it, because, if she did, Robert would get angry. He is always telling her that she is a bad wife because she doesn't smile enough, and she isn't happy enough. He tells me, *"Son, when you get married, make sure your wife can cook, and that she smiles, and puts out."*

I don't know what he means by *puts out,* but whenever he says is, Mom's face goes all tight and her eyes go little and hard.

At night, he tells her that she doesn't show him enough love. Their room is next to mine and the walls are paper thin, so I can hear almost everything. What Robert means by love is that he wants to do the things where they make the noises. I hate the noises.

I hate them even more now that Pastor Wren has started to make them with me.

My hands hurt from where they're gripping the hard wooden bench so tightly.

The bell sounds to let everyone know today's sermon is finished. The lady who rings the bell is weird. Sometimes she speaks in different languages that no one understands and screams and shakes. She says it is God moving through her. It scares me.

I went to visit my cousin a few weeks ago, and we went to his church. His church was nice. I really liked it. It was more like the churches you see on television. Pastor Wren's church is different. He says his church in this community is the right way, and the only true way, but I preferred my cousin's church. They sang hymns I knew, and then in Sunday school afterward, we were given a choice between coloring a scene from the Nativity or making a picture with fabrics and glue.

Our Sunday school is very different.

"Time for the children to follow me. The adults can now go and prepare the food for the afternoon feast," Sister Nancy says.

Nancy is a lady who must be very old, because her hair is white, and her face has more lines than even the back of Mom's hands. Her eyes are small but piercing blue, and when she looks at you, it is as if she can see right inside you. I don't like her, but she doesn't scare me the same way Pastor Wren does.

We stand, and the adults all shuffle to the ends of the pews and wander off in the direction of the kitchens. Once there, the women will start preparing the food, as is their place, according to Pastor Wren, and the men will serve the wine and go and sit outside while they talk and chat until the meal is ready.

The children do one of three things.

Children who are in the choir get to practice and sing with Sister Lucy. The children who aren't in the choir, but don't need special guidance, get to do classes and fun things together.

Then there are the children like me.

We are the ones who are naughty. The ones who have done bad things. We must have extra guidance from Pastor Wren. There are four of us, and we are all boys aged between seven and twelve.

My feet move forward as if of their own accord, as I walk with dread toward the door at the back of the church. The door leads through a long corridor and down five steps into Pastor Wren's private study.

In his study, there are some *very bad things*. He likes to show them to us as an example of what we shouldn't do and what sin is. There are all sorts of terrible pictures of people doing things to one another. The pictures scare me. I hate them.

I hate it more when Pastor Wren takes me into the side room alone, for my special education.

I enter the room and look up to see him already at the head of the desk, waiting for us to take our seats. He smiles at us as if he is just a kind man who wants the best for us. His hair is dark but spattered with a few strands of gray. He is medium height, and skinny, like me, but with a stomach that sticks out.

Mom says it's because Pastor Wren likes to take far too much of the church wine for himself. The last time she said that, Robert smacked her across the face. He told her not to disrespect the church leader, and if he heard anyone say

BRUTAL LIMITS

anything bad about Pastor Wren in our household again, that person would get the belt.

It's another reason I can't tell Mom what Pastor Wren does in that small, dark room. If I do, she will surely tell Robert, and then she'll get the belt, or I'll get the belt. The last time I got the belt, I couldn't sit down for almost a week.

Staring at Pastor Wren, I wait. When he turns to look at me, his mouth lifts in a slow smile.

In that moment, something strange happens. I get a feeling I've never had before. It's like a fire burning deep in my belly. It is a feeling that is so big, my small body can't contain it. It is as if any moment I could explode with it.

My mind starts making connections. Robert rules our house because he's the strongest.

There's a man who comes to church. Tom Bradbury. He is huge. No one dares say anything to him because he's big and strong enough to fight anybody. Tom Bradbury is a sinner. He hangs out at the bikers' club, and he has fun with loose women. Mom says so. Yet no one says anything to Tom Bradbury. No one in our home dares to contradict Robert. Why? Because they are strong. They are scary, and people fear them.

I decide there and then that when I grow up, I'm going to be like Tom Bradbury. I'll find out what you have to do to grow so big and strong and tall, and then I will do it. And when I do, I will stop Pastor Wren from hurting me, or any more boys. I don't care if it takes me a lifetime, I will pay Pastor Wren back for this.

A small smile curves across my mouth as I make a solemn vow to myself and to the God that Pastor Wren says he worships. I vow that when I'm a grown-up, I will get big and strong and find Pastor Wren.

I shall hurt him so badly, he'll never harm another person again.

Chapter One
Honor

THANK GOD THAT WHEN the men left me alone in here, they didn't turn off the light. This place is called the bunker, and that is an apt name. If they'd left me in the dark here, I swear I would have gone crazy.

Fear, sorrow, and anger all vie for supremacy. I'm angry at myself, but also at the men who have put me in this position. Yes, perhaps I lied, but I think about things as I sit alone in this disgusting room, and realize they have no right to act as if I'm the one in the wrong and they're the ones in the right.

Someone along the way messed up, and that someone wasn't me. So what if I signed their stupid contract under a false name? Does it really matter? I doubt any of this is truly legal, anyhow. Even if it's legal, it's hardly moral, and if I wanted to, I could ruin their lives by talking about this. I never had that intention, however. I was just stupidly swayed and tempted by the money when it was offered to me. And if I'm being really, truthfully honest, swayed by the chance to do something that deep down intrigued me.

I can't deny that, however much I might want to. These men have ignited something dark within me. I might like to pretend I'm only in it for the money, but really, my desires match their own far too closely for comfort.

Now, though, I'm truly their prisoner. The game got horribly real. I'm not sure what I can do to make the situation any better for myself. When will I have the chance to attempt to crack their almost impenetrable shells again? Will they close down on me forever this time? I felt as if I made some connection, particularly with Rafferty and Wilder, but now that's all gone.

They all seem angry, but Brody is the angriest of them all.

I pace the bunker and try not to think about the fact that I'm locked in. What if there's a fire? I could die in this place, and no one would come to get me out. Panic starts to rise and claw at my chest and throat. Swallowing hard, I try to take a deep breath.

Panic won't get me anywhere.

Fuck, I've messed up. I thought I'd be safer staying here than out there. I thought this would be better than the alternative of being back on the streets and being hunted by *him* again. My stepfather, Don. Now, though, it's becoming clear I was wrong, yet again. I misjudged these men and the depth of their sadism. I misjudged just how deeply fucked up they are. Who has a bunker like this? No one remotely sane.

What was it they said? This is where they bring *men*? Men who pay to come and be tortured.

From what little they said, that side of things is darker than the sexual stuff they do with the women. At least the women are paid and get some pleasure out of it. I can't deny that. These men might be fucked up, but they certainly know how to give

BRUTAL LIMITS

a good orgasm. The fact that there are men who pay to come here and just be… What? Beaten up? Interrogated?

Oh, my God. Is the stuff the men do sexual, too?

I get a pulse of desire, a faint tingling in my clit. Jesus, I'm as fucked up as they are. Here I am, locked up, and I'm still getting horny thinking about them getting it on with men.

Looking around me as I walk, I sigh and battle tears once more.

God, this room is depressing and so soulless. I can't even say it is like Hell because it's more like a void. Devoid of anything that can give a human sustenance, good or bad. There's no burning inferno, no licking flames and terribleness. But there's nothing good either. It's the banality of the evil in this room that terrifies me. The boring gray walls, concrete floor, hard mattress beds, and that damn hole where I'm supposed to pee. There is no way I can stay here. I need to get myself back into one of the bedrooms somehow.

I pause for a moment. I wonder if I can earn my way back into a bedroom. Maybe I can make a bargain with them?

But how? I have no power at all. They said the safeword is gone. Do they mean that?

Pacing once more, I attempt to think rationally. Rafferty is all about the legalities of this, and right now he's angry, but no way is he actually going to want to keep me here as a hostage, against my will, and let the men with him assault me, which is what it will be if I don't have a safeword.

When he calms down, he's going to want this shit to still be legal.

He's the one I need to try to reason with. I'm happy to let the game go on, but it has to be with the safeword, and with some of the money for me at the end of it. Otherwise, first chance I get, I'll run for real. I don't care if I'm risking my life; I will get out of here. I'll find a boat, and I will leave this cursed island.

First, though, I'll try to reason with Rafferty. If he is the legal mind behind all of this, then he must know what they're doing now is deeply dangerous for them.

Then a thought hits me that has my heart sinking. What if they investigate me and find out who I really am?

Oh, God, what if they contact my stepfather? They wouldn't even have to contact him to cause me problems. If they find out he's a cop, they might realize how dangerous he is.

"Calm down, Honor," I tell myself. "They'll likely just find out he's a supposed hero cop."

I sigh in relief, but it's short lived. If they think my stepdad is a hero cop, then that means they have no option. They'll have to get rid of me.

Shit. Fuck.

My breath catches, and I bend over, trying to take a deep breath and calm myself.

Things are so much worse than I initially believed. If they find out who my stepfather is, and realize he's a senior detective in the LA police force, then these men are going to believe I could get them into deep shit. The only way for that not to happen is for me to disappear.

Would they go that far?

Maybe I ought to come clean right now. Tell them the truth and hope they take pity on me.

Which one would be best to confide in? I'd have thought Asher at the start. I'd been so mistaken when I thought he was the nicest. I think he's possibly evil.

I grind my teeth as something almost akin to hatred surges in me. To think that I believed he could be the one out of them I'd get along with the most. Nice, nerdy boy, I thought. What a joke.

Yeah, Asher is out. Wilder might have helped me, but he looked at me with real disgust in his eyes once they found out I'd been lying. I think Wilder is the most hurt at my actions.

Brody is pissed.

It leaves me back at Rafferty again. I need to try to appeal to Rafferty's sense of decency, and if he doesn't possess any, then at least a sense of self-preservation, by playing into the legalities of all this.

Time seems to stretch, and I have no idea whether I've been in this godforsaken room for long minutes, or short hours. It feels like maybe thirty or forty minutes, but I really have no way of knowing. This is torture. As in actual torture. There's a reason they put prisoners in solitary. Before he became my nemesis, when he was still trying to ingratiate himself with my mother and me, Don told us once that solitary confinement is pretty much the worst thing you can do to a human being.

Particularly if you take away control of their lighting. Plunge someone into the dark in a room all alone, where they can't get out, and just leave them there, and you can send them insane. He laughed when he told us this, and in retrospect, that should have been a warning sign of just how sadistic and vicious the man was.

These men haven't left me in the dark, but they have placed me in solitary confinement. In their own way, they are torturing me. A surge of rage fires within me, and I run to the door and start kicking as hard as I can—though my feet are bare and it hurts me more than the door—pounding with my fists and screaming.

It feels good to let some of this pent-up rage and panic out.

"Let me out, you fuckers," I scream. "Let me fucking out. Leeeeeet meeee ooouuuut."

I stop when some of the adrenaline is worn off, and my hands and feet hurt, making sense seep in. I'm just going to harm myself. I doubt there is anybody nearby to hear me, and even if there is, I doubt they care.

What about Felicity? What's her role in this? Would she give a shit if she realized the men were keeping me here against my will for real now?

At some point, I give up pacing and collapse on the nearest bed. I'm exhausted, but I'm also increasingly thirsty and hungry. Are they going to leave me all night with nothing to drink? God, how did I underestimate their cruelty so wildly?

As I think about it all, my eyes start to drift shut. My adrenaline all gone, exhaustion is winning out.

I drift in and out of a disturbed sleep, with dreams coming and going, none of them pleasant. I jolt awake at the sound of the door.

Brody walks in.

He's the last one I wanted to see. He is the angriest with me out of all of them. In his hands he has a tray, and he places it on the floor. There's a bottle of water, and a bowl with what looks like soup in it, alongside a roll on a plate.

"Eat that and drink the water," he orders. "You need your strength for tomorrow."

Even though he's the last person I want to see, I also can't bear the idea of being alone.

"Wait," I tell him.

He pauses at the door, back to me and shoulders tense.

"I've apologized to you all so many times, and I really am sorry, but you need to understand. I didn't know what to do. I was in a bad situation." I still don't feel I can tell them everything, but at least I can let them know that I was in a lot of trouble. "There was a guy who'd attacked me," I say.

"Yeah, you mentioned your stepfather."

Crap, I did, didn't I, though I didn't give them any details. They don't know what he did or that he's a police officer. I can't be sure how they'll react to that news. I know this is just a lie on top of lies, but it's a partial truth, at least.

"I had to get away from him, so I've been sleeping on the streets, or in train stations or in a bus shelter."

He slowly turns and fixes me with his intense gaze.

"I was scared, okay? And when I was mistaken for the girl you want to play those games with, at first I was horrified. But then when I thought about it, I realized she couldn't have turned up, and I honestly didn't see how it would matter if I signed the contract in her place. I don't think what Rafferty is saying can be right, can it? I don't think the contract is null and void just because I didn't sign in my real name. What kind of a contract is it, anyway? Would it really hold up in court if a woman decided to accuse you guys of something terrible against her?"

His jaw starts to work, and I can see he's thinking.

I'm winging this. I had planned on talking to Rafferty, but now one of them is here, I can't seem to stop myself from spilling all this out.

"All I'm saying is...don't you think you should give me another chance? I could be angry at you and the way you've treated me. I'm not, though. I'm willing to let it all go and start again. I'm begging you, Brody, not to leave me here alone tonight in this place. It's so claustrophobic."

I watch him, wondering which way he's going to go.

"I would never tell anyone about what you do here, I promise you that. And like I say," I push my point, "just how watertight do you really think that legal agreement is?"

I see it. The moment I push too far. It's like a shutter coming down across his face. "The contract is airtight." His voice is calm and cold. "Rafferty knows his shit. There's no way he drew up a contract that wouldn't stand up in court."

I ought to shut up, but I can't seem to stop myself. "All I'm saying is that you can't be sure of that. Any of those women you had here could change their mind a few months down the line and decide to say something."

This might not be my cleverest move yet, but I realize as I'm talking how right I am about it. "They signed waivers, so what? What if some woman says some of the stuff you did with her was outside the parameter of that? People have signed nondisclosures in the past, and then reneged on them. Legally binding documents can get broken, and even if they can't win in a court of law, they could win in the court of public opinion. He said, she said. How could you prove it?"

He turns to face me fully, his hands now balled into fists. "I don't know what your game is, but you need to stop this shit right now. If you think things are bad now, keep this up." He jabs a finger at me. "Don't try to split us up, Honor. You really won't like the consequences. We're as tight as brothers. No one can come between us, especially not some used and abused pussy."

With those final, cruel words, he turns and walks out. The door closes heavily behind him, and the lock slides shut.

Chapter Two
Wilder

I CAN'T SLEEP, AND I know why.

The reason I'm tossing and turning is sitting right now in a bunker, probably scared to death. She fucked up, and at first, I was fuming. Probably angrier than any of the others. The girl got her hooks into me, and I can't deny that. I felt stupid. So, yeah, I grabbed her arm and marched her to that bunker myself. Now, though, it's not sitting right with me.

I've been having dreams again recently. Nightmares about Pastor Wren and what he did to me. The way he took my power. We are doing that to Honor now. The game has never been about that, at least not for me. Yeah, the stuff we do is sick and twisted, and a lot of people would judge us harshly for it, but the most important thing for me is that it's always been consensual. We're entering into dangerous territory here, not only legally and ethically, but emotionally, too.

Asher, for one, might believe he is the tough one among us. The hard one. I know better. That kid's shell is nothing more than a veneer he put in place to hide his soft underbelly so the world can no longer see it. It's still there, though, somewhere. What will it do to him if we truly harm Honor?

I need to talk to Rafferty, but right now he's too angry to see sense. That's the trouble with someone like Rafferty, used to having the world falling at his feet. When things don't go his way, and somebody makes him look a fool the way Honor has, his ego gets hurt. When someone with the kind of God complex Rafferty has finds their ego pricked, they can become irrationally angry.

Brody is livid, too. For different reasons, I believe.

I can't see into their heads, but I've known these guys a long time. I think Brody is angry because he *did* have it figured out. He knew deep down that there was something not right with the girl. The rest of us didn't listen to him, and he's every right to be pissed at us. He's probably also pissed at himself because he let his fears slide and didn't give them enough attention. Now he needs somewhere to place the anger, and so it's all loaded upon Honor.

Trouble is, we are guys with a whole lot of baggage. And now Honor's got all that baggage dumped on her.

I get out of bed and walk out of the bedroom and down the hallway to the office where the monitors are. Pushing open the door, I stop when I see Brody already there, watching them. He's tossing a ball into the air as he watches but catches it in both hands when he notices me.

So, he's not sleeping either. On the screen in front of him is Honor. She's also awake and is curled on her side, softly crying.

"Don't know why she's getting herself in such a state," he says gruffly. "It's not as if we left her in the dark, for fuck's sake."

"Being trapped and locked in is pretty much a basic fear of most people," I tell him.

He gives me the side eye and shakes his head, blowing out a long breath. "She's perfectly fucking safe, and she knows it."

"She absolutely does not fucking know it." I suck in a breath of my own and let an angry one out. "Jesus, Brody, come on. You know. We all *know*."

I don't say anything further. He knows what I'm getting at.

He pushes back his chair and stands, ball in hand as he faces me. "That's a totally different situation."

"Is it? Okay, let's forget about then. What about your military time? You were locked in, and interrogated, and you still have nightmares about it. Nightmares that I've witnessed. So you're going to do the same to her?"

"It's not the same fucking situation." He starts to pace. "She's a fucking liar. She risked everything. And she's a horny little bitch who enjoys it. She probably still wants us to fuck her senseless, no matter what we do to her."

I sigh.

Brody ignores it. "I'm not pussying out on this. If you want to, fine. The bitch is already trying to split us up. She tried to get into my head."

"Well, wouldn't you? She has no clue what we could or couldn't do to her. We've threatened her, and scared her, thrown her into a cell and locked her in. Okay, so we left the light on. She's alone, though, and she can't get out. She doesn't know there're cameras, and that we can see her to ensure she's okay."

I sit in a chair and lean forward, resting my head in my hand as I watch the footage of the dark-haired girl crying.

As much as I hate myself for it, for the weakness, it stirs something in my chest. Maybe I'm a weak motherfucker, but I can't help but empathize.

There's another reason this shit does not sit right with me. We might have twisted tastes, probably born in the abuse we suffered as kids ourselves. However, we've always been adamant that we are not like him. We make sure it's consensual. It's why contracts are signed.

"She's trying to turn us against one another," he says. "From the way you're acting, it seems like she's doing a damn good job. We don't normally argue. We're on the same page most of the time, but here we are." He walks to the corner of the room and starts throwing the ball against the wall, catching it on each rebound. "And if you think for one minute Rafferty will just let her out of there, you can think again."

"Yeah, Rafferty's gonna be an issue."

"And Asher." He shakes his head incredulously and throws the ball again.

"I think Asher is more likely to come around than Rafferty, to be honest. Rafferty feels like a fool, and men like him don't like to be made to feel that way. Thing is, though..." I take a deep breath. "Brody, legally, this could turn into some deep shit."

The ball stops bouncing. Silence fills the room. Brody turns his head to me slowly and narrows his eyes. "Were you in here earlier when I took the food?"

"No," I say truthfully. "Taking a shower. Why?"

"Fuck," he mutters.

"What?" I demand.

Thump. Drop. Catch. Throw. The ball throwing starts up again. *Thump. Drop. Catch. Throw.*

The ball resumes its steady bouncing from the wall to the floor to Brody's hand and back to the wall again.

"It's pretty much exactly what she said to me just now." He shakes his head.

"Well, she's not wrong. It's absolutely fucking ironic that the one levelheaded one among us is possibly the one who is going to blow everything up." The more I think about it, the more I wonder if there's something deeper going on here, and it's not just the fact that Rafferty feels stupid, but maybe he's got feelings involved somehow. After all, he was the one who took her V card.

"Look, I don't want to think about this shit anymore. She deserves whatever is fucking coming her way, and then some." Brody sets his jaw in a way that tells me I won't move him any farther right now. "Let's leave things for now and see how things shake out tomorrow."

Brody drops the ball to the floor. He walks by, clapping me on the shoulder, and closes the door quietly behind him.

Sitting back in my chair, I run my hands through my hair as I watch the girl on the bed silently cry.

Chapter Three
Honor

SOMEHOW, I FINALLY fall asleep. I have no idea for how long, but I wake with swollen eyes and a pounding head. Despite my situation, my dreams were a mix of nightmares but also erotic fragments. I woke up twice in the night aroused, slick, and wet, and in the end, I rubbed myself and came, just to get some relief.

I sit up and blink under the electric light, utterly unsure of what time it is.

My stomach rumbles, and I look around in panic, trying to see if there is any way to guess the time. What if they've forgotten about me and just left me here?

What if someone came to the compound and took them away for some reason, and now I'm left to die?

My chest tightens, and I struggle to get air in as the dark reality of my situation hits me.

I can't breathe.

Fuck, I really can't breathe. It's like the air won't go into my lungs.

I clutch at the blanket in desperation and fall off the bed onto my hands and knees. I slide my hand onto my chest as the other arm props me up on the floor.

I gasp and splutter, tears filling my eyes as the door opens.

Rafferty stares at me with his eyes wide.

"What the fuck you doing?" he asks.

I can't answer him because I can't speak. Finally, probably at the sight of him, my lungs relax, the spasm dying down, and I'm sucking in blessed air.

I cough and choke and finally breathe in and out a few times before I collapse on the floor and start to sob.

Holy hell, what was that?

"Get the fuck up."

I don't even respond to the harsh command because I'm not capable of standing even if I wanted to.

Heavy footsteps scuff across the floor, and Rafferty's boots fill my line of vision. For some reason, my mind focuses on the mundane, and I wonder why he's wearing such different shoes than normal.

"I said get the fuck up." He grabs my arm and pulls me to standing.

I'm still struggling to breathe properly, so I let him manhandle me. I'm as limp as a rag doll and have no fight in me at all.

"What the fuck is wrong with you?" he asks.

"I don't know. I couldn't breathe," I tell him.

"Probably a panic attack," he says with little consideration for how horrific what I've just been through was.

God, he's so cold.

"Don't you feel anything for me?" I ask. "When we made love, we seemed to have a moment where it felt as if there was a connection between us...that you felt it, too."

"Made love?" He barks out a laugh. Then turns deadly serious. "Don't romanticize us."

"Oh, excuse me if I thought for a brief period of time that any of you have beating hearts or are human in any way at all."

"Yeah, that was a mistake."

"Where are we going?"

"Breakfast."

"Good. I'm ravenous," I say.

He looks at me, and his mouth tips up into a diabolical smirk. Honestly, that smile chills me. It's almost evil. I've never seen him wear an expression like it before.

"You'll be full, all right, don't you worry. But before we go over to the resort, there's something you need to have."

I frown. "Oh, what's that?"

"Open your mouth."

Unease runs through me. "Why?"

"Open your fucking mouth, Honor. If you're staying here, you'll do it."

His tone doesn't give me any room for argument. Feeling self-conscious, I part my lips and stick out my tongue slightly.

He has something in his hands. A rectangular foil packet. He presses something out of it and then places the item on my tongue. It's tiny and sugar-coated.

"Swallow," he instructs.

I want to spit it out and demand to know if he's drugging me, but my body is no longer my own—at least not for the next five days. If I'm to stand any chance of getting off this island with a large sum of cash in my pocket—or at least in my bank account—I have to do whatever they say. It's what I've sold my soul for. I just have to keep reminding myself that no matter what they put me through, there's no way it'll be as bad as what my stepfather will do to me if he were to find me.

I swallow.

"Good girl," he tells me.

"What was that?"

He presses the foil packet into my palm. "It's the progesterone only pill."

"You gave me a contraceptive pill?"

"If you're going to be with us for any more time, we don't want to take any chances."

I think of what I know of the pill. "But...doesn't it take at least seven days to work?"

"Not this one. I assume you're not on the first day of your period?"

He arches an eyebrow. It's a snarky remark. He knows full well that I'm not. After all, I'm naked, and that shit would have gotten very messy very quickly.

I don't bother to answer, and he continues.

"This pill will start to work within two days, no matter what point of your cycle you take it in. You need to take it within a three-hour window every day, though, for it to work. Think you can manage that?"

I scowl. "I'm not a child."

"Good to hear it. Now, let's go."

I put the packet down on the mattress and wrap my arms around my torso. "Can I have something to wear first?"

"No."

BRUTAL LIMITS

I'm fully aware that keeping me naked is all part of his powerplay. It leaves me feeling vulnerable.

He turns and marches back to the doorway, so I follow and step out into the bright sun. My eyes tear from the light, but I quickly get used to it.

There's a short hike across the island, back to the resort, and my bare feet seem to find every sharp stone and stick. I hop from foot to foot, trying to avoid the discomfort, but it doesn't do any good. I'm hugely aware of my nakedness, too. What if the other members of staff see me? But then I remind myself of the games these men play, and the sort of people who come here, and realize that seeing a dirty, naked girl being hauled across the island probably isn't anything they haven't seen before.

Rafferty's tight grip on my upper arm doesn't loosen as he marches me into the building, down one of the plush corridors, and into a dining room I haven't been in before.

The guys are all lined up.

What is this?

"Get on your knees," Rafferty orders.

I don't move.

"If you don't get on your fucking knees, I'll get you on our plane and back to the mainland and hand you over to the cops."

It's got to be an empty threat. Surely. Do they know about my stepfather? As much as I'm fearful of what these men might do to me, it doesn't even compare to what he might do if he finds me. Despite the cruelty I know Rafferty and the others are capable of, I don't believe for one second that they'd kill me. Honestly, I don't think they'd physically harm me either, other than perhaps with a good spanking or scratched feet from running.

That knowledge goes some way to calming me, though my heart continues to race. I rake my gaze over the men, searching their faces for any sign that they may be softening toward me.

Asher stares at me from behind his black framed glasses. His gaze is hard and unreadable. As I watch, he clenches and unclenches his fists, as though he's warming up his fingers for what comes next. Brody barely seems to look at me. He's toying with the dog tags he wears around his neck, and his gaze is somewhere over my head. Wilder—the biggest and roughest of the four of them—folds his arms over his chest. He tilts his head to one side, as though still assessing me, and his long hair falls over his shoulder. I catch his eye and silently plead with him to forgive my lies. Before they'd caught me out, I'd started to wonder if perhaps he was catching feelings for me. Something about the way he'd held me and touched me made me feel like our hearts were reaching out to one another. I want desperately for him to understand that I'm still the same person and whatever mistakes I'd made had never been malicious. They'd been born out of a place of fear and desperation, not anger or hate.

"Please, can I—"

I'd been intending to plead my case once more, but Rafferty's voice silences me.

"Enough. You're here for breakfast, aren't you?"

My stomach rumbles, and hot acid burns up the back of my throat.

My gaze darts between them, trying to understand where this is going. I am starving, but I can't see any sign of a meal being delivered. It's just me and the four men.

"Yes," I say hesitantly. "I am."

"Then get on your knees."

Realizing I don't have much choice, I lower myself to the floor. My heart is pounding.

Rafferty walks a slow circle around me.

"How many cocks can you suck, Honor? One after the other? How much cum can you swallow?"

It dawns on me that this is what he meant by breakfast. I won't be seeing a buffet any time soon.

My voice leaves my mouth in a breathy whisper. "As many and as much as you need me to."

An actual, real smile curls the corners of his lips. "Good girl. That's what I like to hear. You're learning."

His hands go to his suit pants, and he pops open the button and pulls down the zipper. He reaches into the gap and frees himself, so his cock bobs out to meet me. It's only a foot from my face.

Despite what I've been up to over the past few days, I still feel like I'm inexperienced in all matters of sex. This is all new to me, and the prospect of sucking each of them off—assuming that's what's expected of me—and swallowing them makes me tremor inside. What if my jaw gets too sore? What if I gag? What if so much cum makes me sick? I don't want to show myself up, and I don't want to let them down either.

If I tell them I can't, and I want it to stop, will they?

Rafferty steps closer. "Open up, princess."

I drop my lower jaw. The smooth, firm head of his cock passes my lips and slides across my tongue. The musky scent of him fills my nostrils, and I draw in a deep breath through my nose. God, he smells good. The thought sends a tingling down through my lower belly and warms between my thighs.

I wrap my fingers around the base of him and lift my eyes to meet Rafferty's.

He nods approvingly. "That's right. I like a little eye contact while I fuck your face."

I take him as far in I as can manage, and he hits the back of my throat. I feel myself start to gag, and I suck air in through my nose, fighting it.

He grips my hair to hold me in place and laughs. "You can gag all you want. Can't beat the feeling of a throat closing around my cock."

Tears prick my eyes. He shunts his hips forward, going deeper, and I lose my control and my throat closes around him.

"Ah, fuck, yes," he groans.

To my relief, he pulls himself out a couple of inches, giving me a moment to recover. I don't want to let him down, though, so I use my hand to pleasure him, pumping his length until I'm ready to sink down once more.

I'm hugely aware of the other three watching, waiting their turn. Is this turning them on? As much as I don't want to admit it, I'm growing slick between my thighs. I reach my hand to my pussy but receive a sharp slap to my shoulder.

"Don't touch yourself," Rafferty snaps. "This isn't for you."

The smack was hard enough to sting. I whimper and squeeze my thighs together, desperate for some pressure there.

I remember what he said, though, and force myself to focus on him. We've reached a rhythm now as his thrusts grow faster and his dick gets even harder in my mouth. It's like iron. I'm sure he's bruising my throat, but I don't complain. I stare up at him with my tear-filled eyes and use my lips and tongue as best I can.

His face tenses and then screws up in pleasure. He lets out a groan, and hot semen gushes down my throat in spurt after spurt. I hardly have the chance to think about swallowing—there's nowhere else it can go.

His dick grows soft between my lips, and he releases his hold on my hair. I drop to my haunches, gasping for breath.

Rafferty's fingers brush my cheek. "You did well," he tells me.

Fresh tears spring to my eyes. This is the first bit of affection any of them has shown me since they found out about my lie, and I want to press my cheek to his palm and beg for more.

I almost hate myself for it, but I discover I want to please him. I want to please all of them. I want to make my lie up to them so they can see I'm not this conniving person they've made me out to be in their minds.

Rafferty tucks himself away, and Asher steps forward.

I swallow, hard, fresh nerves fluttering in my stomach. Asher is cold—even colder than Rafferty has been to me—and he's the one I fear the most now. How ironic that, at first, I thought he might be my savior in all this.

"Glad Rafferty got you all warmed up," he says. "Now it's my turn."

Within seconds, I'm faced with his dick. Like Asher himself, it's long and slender, but perfectly formed. He holds himself, so I don't need to use my hands, and he uses his other hand to cup my chin.

"Lick it first," he tells me. "Wrap that pretty little tongue around me."

I do as he says, flattening my tongue to lick the head and then the length, like I've just been presented with the world's tastiest popsicle. He gazes down at me with cool eyes, but that crazy little part of my brain that wants to please is hoping that if I do this well enough, those cool eyes might warm. His hold on my chin doesn't ease, and as I cover the head with my lips and then press my tongue to his slit, he sucks air in over his teeth.

"Ah, fuck."

I withdraw slightly, worried I've done something wrong, but he shakes his head.

"Keep going."

I do, alternating bobbing up and down his length with forcing my tongue into his slit. I don't know if it hurts him, but, if it does, he likes it. Our movements increase in speed, then Asher's hand moves from my chin to wrap around my throat. He squeezes his fingers enough to add pressure, but not enough to close my airways. Considering his cock is in my mouth, I'm thinking he won't risk me biting down on it to set myself free. My airways are constricted enough to make me lightheaded, however, and my brain takes on a state of wooziness, almost as though I'm about to fall asleep or perhaps had too much to drink. I wouldn't tell Asher—because I'd never want to encourage him—but it's not an unpleasant sensation.

From somewhere to my right, I hear Brody say, "I'm getting my dick wet before it's my turn."

I'm aware of movement behind me, but it's hard to keep track when Asher is fucking my face and half strangling me. But then fingers touch my pussy, and I squeak around Asher's cock. Surprise instantly morphs to pleasure as Brody fingers me then positions himself, kneeling behind me. Roughly, he pushes himself into me, even as I still have my lips clamped around Asher's dick. A slow roll of pleasure undulates through me, and though he's rough, I'm already wet from sucking off the others. I come to the conclusion he's happy to fuck me instead of getting me to suck him.

I try to focus on the cock between my lips, wanting to please Asher, but it's hard to keep up my rhythm when I have Brody fucking me and Asher still choking me. I'm trapped between them. They don't touch my clit, and the needy little nub aches, desperate for attention. I don't dare touch myself—I don't want to get in any more trouble. I wonder if it's possible to come from the pounding Brody is giving my pussy, but I don't feel like any of this is being done for me. They're using my body like a fuck-toy, and I'm letting them.

Asher's fingers tighten around my throat, and his movements grow faster. Suddenly, he holds himself deep, and hot salty fluid spurts down my throat. I gag, but he holds me still, his cock jerking in my mouth, releasing those few extra gushes of cum. Growing softer, he steps away, and my throat and mouth are empty.

Behind me, Brody pulls out of my pussy, though I know he hasn't reached his climax yet.

I slump, gasping for breath, bracing myself up with my hands so I don't drop face first onto the floor. This isn't over yet.

Brody moves around to stand in front of me. My pussy feels empty now he's no longer inside me, and my inner muscles clench as though searching for something to grip onto it.

"Fuck me," I manage to gasp. "Please, someone fuck me. I need to come, too."

The men exchange glances

I'm pathetic, and I know it.

"Please, I want you to punish me."

I glance over at where Wilder is still waiting, begging him with my eyes. His massive cock has always slightly terrified me, but now I find myself a desperate ball of desire. I'm sopping wet from Brody readying me.

I want it.

In front of me, Brody grips the base of his cock and presses the head to my lips. The scent of my own musk washes over me.

"See how wet my dick is? That's all you, Pandora. Your hungry little cunt got me soaked. Now lick it off."

His eyes glitter. He clearly still hasn't forgiven me, but I so badly want him to. I wish I could change my mindset and tell them all to fuck off, but I can't. Some part of me wants to belong to something. I've been alone for so long, and I'd thought I might have found something special among these intense men and this beautiful place. I wish more than anything I'd owned up to who I was at the start and asked if I could play anyway. They might have said yes and simply had a new contract written, but I couldn't go back now.

I lick the head of his cock, lapping off my own cream, together with his salty precum. My pussy throbs, and I slip my eyes shut as I renew my enthusiasm on his dick, humming and moaning my enjoyment.

"Fuck," Asher says. "She really loves cock. You sure she was a virgin when she came here?"

Rafferty snorts. "Yeah, she was definitely a virgin. I took her cherry."

Brody jerks his hips forward. "Fuck, she's good at that."

Even though they're talking about me like I'm not here, I relish their encouragement. I lift a hand to cup Brody's balls, gently squeezing and rolling, then I slide my fingers farther back, pressing that sensitive spot between his asshole and balls. I briefly wonder how he'd react if I was the one to push a finger inside him? Would he be one of those guys who'd get all funny about it, thinking anything anal automatically made him gay, or would he be into it?

Experimentally, I move farther back, the curves of his pert ass brushing my fingers. I graze his hole with my fingertip, and he grunts and shoves his dick deeper down my throat. It takes me a moment to readjust my mouth and tongue around his length.

I push just the tip in, and his breathing grows harsher. "Ah, fucking hell."

He doesn't tell me to stop, though. A strange sense of power rises inside me. Okay, this is new. I literally have all of Brody's most sensitive spots under my control, and even though he could still do whatever he wanted to me, I like that this man who seems so held together ninety-nine percent of the time literally looks like he's about to lose his mind because of my mouth and fingers.

I edge my finger in deeper, feeling his walls clamp around the digit, and wriggle it around. I don't know what I'm doing, but I must accidentally hit the right spot as his entire body goes rigid.

"Oh, Jesus," he curses. "Oh, fuck, yes."

He spills himself inside my mouth, and I hold my finger deep until he finishes shuddering around me.

He seems to go weak, and I remove my hand. "Christ, Honor."

My heart swells, knowing I've affected him.

I squeeze my thighs together and squirm, hating that I can get wet from this. Heat floods through my veins and condenses in my pussy. Fuck. These men have locked me in a fucking dungeon, and yet one hint of getting dick from them turns me into a little whore.

"You still want to get fucked, Snow?" Wilder asks me.

My pussy throbs in response. I nod.

"Lie back, then. We're doing this here and now."

The floor is cool beneath my body, but I do as he says. I feel so raw and vulnerable lying here like this. My chest is flushed with heat, my nipples hard.

Wilder settles himself between my legs. He spreads my thighs and then puts his hands on the insides of them to press them wider. My pussy opens as though greeting him, the wet, pink folds leading to darkness. I've already had Brody's cock inside me, so I'm stretched and ready.

He undoes his jeans and yanks them down his hips.

The glint of metal at the end of his cock catches my eye, and I suck in a breath. Oh, God. Can I really do this? A flash of fear and panic goes through me.

He grips his huge dick in his hand and leans over me. He rubs the cool metal against my clit, and I buck my hips. It's like fireworks going through me, bright dots of light flashing in front of my eyes. Oh, Jesus. I'm so turned on; I feel like my entire body might split apart at any moment. Is it possible to die from the pleasure of an orgasm? I'd put money on it being possible.

Of course, I'm young and healthy and I'm quite sure that isn't going to happen to me, no matter how much I feel it might.

He rubs his cock up and down my slit a couple of times, coating his head and the piercing in my slick wetness. "Exhale, Honor. Slow and steady?"

I'm longing to be filled, desperate for it. I want him inside me, and I want to know how that piercing will feel against my inner walls, but as he presses forward and applies that extra pressure needed to breach my pussy, a flash of panic takes hold.

"Wilder, please! I don't think I can."

"Yes, you can. Your cunt can fit a baby's head, so it sure as hell can take my cock."

I'm pretty sure that during childbirth, a woman's body releases all kinds of endorphins and other hormones that allow us to stretch that much.

"I don't have enough experience. I'll be too tight. You'll hurt me."

His eyes darken. "After your lies, maybe you deserve a little hurt?"

Had I hurt him? Is that what he's trying to say? I'd betrayed his trust and hurt him, and now he was going to use his monster cock to repay me. I deserve it, too, don't I? I shouldn't have lied.

They've given me a beautiful place to stay, amazing food, and incredible sex, and I repaid them by putting their home and business in jeopardy.

There's something else I still haven't told them, and my heart clenches. Aren't I still putting them in danger? My stepfather is high up in the police. He's well respected. What if he somehow manages to track me down here and realizes what this place is used for? He could easily expose all the guys and have this place shut down. I'm not sure exactly what laws they're breaking—though I guess keeping me in that bunker constituted false imprisonment—but I know my stepfather well enough to know that actual breaking of a law won't matter. He'll set them all up for something, if he wants. I won't put it past him hiding a huge amount of drugs somewhere on the island and having them sent down for that, or even hiding a body here and making it look like the guys are responsible.

I can't tell them, though, can I? If they know about my stepfather being a cop, they'll throw me off the island for sure, and then I'll not only be penniless, but I'll also be at the mercy of him finding me.

"Hold her down," Wilder says to Asher and Brody. He looks at me, as though waiting for me to protest, but I don't. I reached my arms out as though in a star shape, and Asher twines his fingers through my right hand, and Brody through my left.

Wilder's upper lip curls as he presses my legs even farther apart and edges inside me another inch. The burn is very real, and I gasp and pull back on where the other two men are holding me. Rafferty stands over us, as though he's about to shout directions.

To Wilder's credit, he pauses again and allows my body to adjust to the invasion. Then he reaches between us and thumbs my clit. I let out a breathy cry and lift my hips, this time encouraging him to push deep. My pussy is stretched wide around his cock, which has the girth of a soda can, but it's also hot and silky smooth, and ridged with veins. Then there's the metal piercing, and as I arch my pelvis, I'm sure I can feel it rubbing against my inner walls.

"You want it now, Honor, huh?" he growls. "You want my fat cock inside you."

"Yes," I gasp. "I want it."

He grabs my hip with his other hand and shunts forward. This time, he slides so much deeper, and I cry out.

"Fuck me. Look at that." His gaze is fixed on where our bodies meet.

My thighs are spread wide, while his huge form is supported above me. I'm so full, my eyes roll back with pleasure.

He pulls out slowly, and I'm almost bereft, but then he shunts back in, and my tits bounce.

He hits a spot deep inside me, and I know the piercing has done its job. It's like an electric shock going through me, every nerve ending alight with pleasure. I jerk and shudder, my pussy clenching around his girth.

"Oh, oh, God, oh, fuck," I cry.

Wilder just holds still, his gaze now fixed on my face. He's basically just letting me get off on his cock, hardly even having to do anything other than strum my clit and hold himself in that key spot.

Brody and Asher keep me pinned down, and I'm impaled on Wilder. Rafferty's hard again, fisting himself as he stands over us. Always the master.

My climax takes over, and my eyes roll, my toes curling. My orgasm rolls over me again and again, and I'm a shaking, shuddering mess.

Finally, I fall still, breathing hard, my heartrate still hammering.

Wilder starts to fuck me again. Now I've orgasmed, my pussy is slicker and taking him is easier. It still feels like a massive invasion, though, and I'm pretty sure I won't be able to sit down for a day or two.

He fucks me hard, his face a contorted expression of pain and pleasure. I want to touch him, to run my hands over his thick muscles, to claw my nails through his hair and over his back, but I'm still pinned down.

Wilder pulls out of me before he comes—I admire his self-control and can't imagine many men would be able to stop at that point. For a second, I think he's doing it to avoid getting me pregnant, since the contraceptive pill won't have started working yet, but he moves quickly for such a big man, hauling himself up my body so he ends up straddled across my chest. He grips my chin in one hand while his cock is in the other.

"Open up."

Obediently, I part my lips, and he pumps himself a couple more times before a stream of milky fluid spurts from his slit. Much of it hits my lips and tongue, and the rest jets onto my cheeks and in my hair. I gasp and blink. It wasn't what I'd expected.

He doesn't so much as thank me before climbing off. I think I'm done, but then Rafferty's cum rains down on me, hitting my bare breasts and stomach.

Brody and Asher release me, and I just lie there, stunned.

"Get up," Rafferty says, putting himself away. "I hope you enjoyed your breakfast."

I blink, unable to speak. I'm not hungry anymore, that's for sure.

"Come on, up."

I manage to push myself to sitting. I know I'm going to be sore tomorrow. I hope I'll be able to walk. I glance between my thighs, half expecting to see my pussy still stretched wide, but it isn't. Thank God for that.

Will they give me something real to eat now? I'm not sure I could even stomach anything.

I long for the soft bed I'd been in previously and would kill for a hot shower. Surely they'll allow me such things now?

Rafferty grabs my upper arm and hauls me the rest of the way up.

"Let's go."

"Where am I going?" I dare ask.

"Back to your room."

My heart lifts with hope. But he must have seen my expression, as he snorts.

"Not that one. You think we're done with you already? Not a chance."

I catch Wilder's eye as I leave, and for the first time since he found out about my lie, I see something akin to pity there.

Chapter Four
Asher

MY FINGERS FLY OVER the keyboard.

Who is this girl?

Okay, maybe Honor just wants the money, but then so has every other girl who's come before her, and none of them have felt the need to lie about who they are. Plus, they'd always tapped out long before we've put them through anything like we've put Honor through over the past twenty-four hours.

Any sane person would have run by now, and yet she just takes us, over and over again. Yes, maybe greed is playing a part in it and she wants to be a millionaire, but she doesn't seem that kind of person. I remember how she arrived here, with barely any belongings and in shabby clothes. Her hair was a mess, and she hadn't been wearing a scrap of makeup. She certainly didn't come across as someone who gave a shit about money.

Yet, she must be, for her to have lied about her identity and signed that contract. Admittedly, she hadn't really known what she was getting herself into when she signed it, but it's pretty fucking clear now, and she's still wet for us and decided to stay to finish this, but without her safeword.

She liked the sex. All of it, before and after we found out she'd been lying. Despite all her protests, that much was clear. Maybe the degradation didn't go down so well with her, but it still got her wet. But again, is the sex enough for her to put up with all the other shit we're throwing at her?

I tap my fingers against my lips.

There's a story here, and I'm determined to find out what it is, even if I've got the feeling the others may not want to know. Though they're acting as though they hate her, I've seen the ways they look at her when they think no one is watching. Before they found out she'd been lying, there had been some moments where they'd been genuinely affectionate toward her. I hadn't seen that before either. The women who'd come before Honor had never had her vulnerability. Even when they'd been fighting us off, it was obvious they were acting. They'd come here wanting to get fucked by four men, wanting us to take them by force, and we'd always known it had been an act.

With Honor, it was different, and we all felt it.

I'm the only one whose heart is truly hard.

Sometimes I wonder if I was always like this. I don't have memories of my life before Pastor Wren came into it, though I know I existed. I've seen photographs of me as a child at three, five, seven years old, and in the photographs I'm smiling and my eyes are lit up. Was I acting then? I can't imagine how it feels to genuinely experience an emotion other than anger or hate or jealousy...or shame.

Yes, shame is the worst of them. Deep down, I think it's where the other three stem from.

I tell myself that if I feel those negative emotions then I can't be completely broken. There's no light without dark. No warm without cold. Somewhere, buried deep inside me, there must be the capacity for something good. I just have no idea how to reach it.

I shake my head at myself. Not that I want to reach it. Positive emotions mean vulnerability, and I'm all done with being vulnerable. Fuck that shit. I've seen what it does to a person. When I look at those photographs of me as a kid, I feel nothing but pity for the boy I once was. He loved. He trusted. He put himself in the hands of people who should have cared for him, and instead they did the exact opposite.

Though I can't remember being him, I know I'm nothing like the boy in those photos, because if someone tried to do the things to me now that they did to that little boy, I'd slit their fucking throat.

A small smile tweaks the corners of my lips.

I still intend on slitting that person's throat, only it won't be done fast. Oh, no. I'll make him suffer in ways he's never even thought about. I'll dismantle his body, piece by piece, starting with his balls, and I'll do it over days, if not weeks. I'll cauterize his injuries to ensure he doesn't bleed out, and I'll use smelling salts to keep him conscious, and I'll force him to watch as he's reduced to little more than a head and torso. Then I'll work on his face.

A cold rage settles inside me, and I grit my teeth and tense my muscles.

We're closer now, closer than we've ever been.

Once that job is done, my reason for existing all these years will be over. No more pain, no more anger, no more shame. I haven't told the others, because I know they'd try to stop me, try to tell me I have a reason to live, but I don't.

I'll be happy to greet the darkness and know I don't have to wake to another day in a world like this one.

The only positive thing I have in my life is pleasure, and I only get that from sex. I think the others know that, which is why they've helped to bring women like Honor over to the island. They think if they give me enough of what I want that I'll somehow change.

It's not enough.

I refocus on my laptop. Honor's true identity is bound to be somewhere on the web. Everyone leaves a trail of themselves online, even if they think they are being careful.

I type her name in: Honor Harper. And hit enter.

Nothing. Crap, she was using a fake name. What did she say her real surname was? I search my memory, so stressed it takes me a moment to recall.

Armitage. That's what she said. Might be a lie, too, but I'll try. I also have her picture, and facial recognition can do the rest. Unless the girl has access to the best forgers and hackers to erase her past, which I highly doubt, I'm going to find her, whatever her name may or may not be.

I upload the photograph of her onto the dark web, together with the name Honor Armitage, and wait.

She was being truthful in that moment. Her name *is* Honor Armitage. Now I have her info, including her correct social security number, I can dig deep into her past. Page after page of entries come up.

There she is as a teenager, linked to her school, where she'd entered a spelling bee and it had been covered by a local paper. And again, when she'd done a fun run and had placed for her sex and age. There is a photograph of her as a gawky teen, her dark hair pulled back into a tight ponytail, grinning at the camera, a gap between her two front teeth. I would guess she was about thirteen in the picture, and she hadn't yet grown into the beautiful young woman that she's become, but the promise of her beauty is there.

I keep scrolling.

A more recent article gives me reason to pause.

'...surviving daughter, Honor Armitage...'

Her mother had died, fairly recently, according to the article. She'd been drinking and had fallen down the stairs and broken her neck.

I experience a strange sensation in my chest, a tightening of my lungs. What is that? Empathy? Do I actually feel sorry for Honor?

I almost laugh at myself. So, her mother died in an accident? So fucking what? We've all been through a hell of a lot worse than that.

Still, I can't help but wonder if that's the reason she's here. Is it connected to her mother's death? I keep reading...

...widower, Detective Don Bowen, spoke of his wife's death... 'her loss has broken me as a man, but I'll do everything within my power to ensure her daughter, Honor, will be taken care of'...

That word jumps out of the laptop screen at me.

Detective.

Fuck. Fuck, fuck, fuck.

I jump to my feet and pace the room, the corner of my thumb clamped between my teeth as I chew at the dry skin. Honor's father is a detective? No, he isn't her father, he used the words, *her daughter*. No father would say that. They have different surnames, too. This must be a stepfather. Is this some kind of conspiracy? Is she working for him, and he sent her here to uncover what we're doing? Is that why she used a fake surname?

But that doesn't make sense. Technically, we aren't breaking any laws. Maybe morally—and it certainly won't be any good for our reputations if what we actually do here goes public—but enough for a detective to not only be interested, but to send his stepdaughter here to get fucked every way since Sunday? No one in their right mind would do that.

Then I remember. Holy crap. *She told us!*

Back when we first found her out about her lying, she mentioned being on the run from a man, and she said her stepfather. She didn't say he was a detective, but she said he was the reason she ran. What the fuck has he done to her?

I know I need to tell the others, but the thought of throwing another bomb in the middle of our situation doesn't sit easy with me. They're already antsy about Honor, and it bothers me that them being upset with her puts them all in a bad mood. Even after they'd all fucked her at breakfast, it hadn't done anything for their joviality. I'm used to being the sourpuss among us, and I find I miss the comradery of the others jesting with each other.

Should I keep this to myself?

Could I?

I wonder if it will do any harm. It's not as though we're letting anyone else on the island while Honor is here, anyway. Once we're done with her, and she gets her money—whether it's the full amount or the two hundred grand—she'll be out of our lives for good. We never bring women back here once they've played with us. None of them have ever *wanted* to come back here. I suspect I have something to do with that. The primal play is one thing, but I like breath play. I like to wrap my hands around their throats as they're close to orgasm and squeeze and squeeze and squeeze. Having that power at my fingertips makes me come like nothing else. I love seeing the panic in their eyes, the terror that I'm not going to release them in time, and they feel that fear at the same time they climax. Because they come both terrified and with their brains low on oxygen, that climax is the most intense of their lives. Nothing else will ever come close.

I think that scares them as much as the possibility that I might kill them. I like to think that I wouldn't—or at least that the others would step in before it got that far—but I never really care if they live or die. It isn't like they mean anything to me. They're just another fuck. Another source of entertainment for the four of us.

Life means nothing. It's fleeting. Practically a dream.

I might not want to, but ultimately, I know I have to tell Rafferty. It's not worth his wrath if something were to happen and he discovered I'd withheld information from him.

As usual, I find him in his office.

All work and no play, and all that crap. But then I remind myself that we always make time to play.

He's alone. For that, at least, I'm grateful. I don't think Brody and Wilder have been thinking straight about this girl. They've got their emotions all tangled up. I know Brody is pissed with us for not listening to him when Honor first arrived. He'd picked up on something not being right immediately. I guess I can't blame him.

"Rafferty, we have a problem."

He turns to face me. "What now? Don't tell me it's Honor again."

I grimace. "It's Honor again."

"What the fuck has she done now?"

"It's not so much what she's done and more to do with who she is. Actually, that's not quite true. It's more to do with who her family is."

Rafferty lets out a sigh and sinks into his chair. He laces his fingers in his dark hair and leans back. "Go on, then. Tell me."

"Honor's mother died, and do you remember she mentioned her stepfather to us?"

He frowns.

"When she was begging our forgiveness, she said she was running from a man, we asked who, she said her stepfather. We didn't follow that up. Pretty big ball to drop, if you ask me."

Rafferty eyes me curiously. "Okay," he says slowly, waiting for me to get the fuck to the point. "I take it there is more? A reason this is coming back up now."

I nod. "Her stepfather is a detective."

Rafferty's eyes narrow. "A detective. Is that something we need to worry about?"

"Honestly, I'm not sure. It looks as though he is well respected. He's done well with his career. A veritable hero from what I can see."

"Yet his stepdaughter is currently on an island with us." Rafferty rubs his fingers across his mouth. "She says she's trying to get away from him, so either…" He pauses, and he is calculating, thinking, doing that thing he does where he lays out all the possible future possibilities and ranks their probabilities. It has helped build his fortune to even greater heights. "Either she really is on the run from him, which means he's looking for her. Or it's a setup. Do we think he knows where she is?"

I bark a cold laugh. "Would you let your stepdaughter come to a place like this if you knew exactly what happened to them? If she is here at his behest, he's a piece of shit. If she's running from him...he's a piece of shit. Either way, her stepfather is a cop, a hero cop, but something about him is off."

"Fuck me." He rakes a hand over his face. "No wonder she's not fighting this. Fighting *us*, more. Even now, with all we've thrown at her, she's been compliant. Not the way she was at first. I thought she'd have fought us. For real. Instead, once we threatened her with throwing her off the island, all the fight went out of her."

I arch an eyebrow. "Yeah, right? And right now, despite everything, she wants to be here. I can tell. If we gave her that old room back and offered her the old deal, she'd snap it up. Hell, I bet she'd stay if we offered her the old room and a bit of friendliness and nothing more."

I realize then how lonely she is. It covers her like a cloak, and it takes one who is also truly alone to recognize it. Her being lonely, though, doesn't make her less dangerous to us, and I can't let these seemingly newfound emotions cloud my judgement.

All that matters, all that has to matter, is finding the Pastor and ending him. I can't let a little scrap of prettiness like Honor come between that and cloud things.

Rafferty rises to his feet. "I'm going to have to talk to her."

I snort. "What's the fucking point? She'll just lie again, won't she? How can we trust anything that comes out of her mouth?"

He knows I have a point.

"We make it so she can't lie."

A smirk forms on his face. "We know how to torture people, don't we?"

Even I'm surprised at hearing that from Rafferty. "You want to torture her? Like we do to the men?"

The sick fucks who come here put themselves through hell at our hands. Sleep deprivation. Water boarding.

"No, not like that. I think we can have a lot more fun with her."

Chapter Five
Honor

THE SOUND AT THE BUNKER door has me bracing. I'm shocked when it's Rafferty who walks in. For some reason, he's the last one I'd been expecting.

He closes the door behind him softly, controlled, but the set of his jaw tells me he's still pissed at me.

Watching me closely, he folds his arms over his chest, leans against the wall, angles his head, and considers me. "Hello, pretty little liar."

I sigh and feel myself shutting down more. At first, when I realized what being their plaything entailed, I had found it exhilarating. Now, I'm just scared, hungry, and sad. I can't tell them to go fuck themselves because they'll dump me on the mainland with no money, and I bet Don will find me in a matter of days.

Looking at Rafferty, for the first time I feel something akin to hate. An anger surges in me, and I grind my teeth.

"See that?" he says conversationally as he unfolds his arms, pushes off the wall, and walks to me. "That's what I want to see more of."

Hatred?

He's so handsome up close. Magnetic, too. He's big built, and sometimes it's easy not to notice because Wilder is a giant, but Rafferty is tall and powerful, with amazing muscles filling out his close-fitting shirt.

"That fight. I want it back."

I blink at him, surprised. I thought they simply wanted me to be their little rag doll now, so they could punish me.

"I think it might be gone for good," I tell him. Tears fill my eyes, and I blink them away angrily.

"I know your stepfather is a hero cop in Los Angeles." His voice is soft, but I flinch as if he hit me.

Shit.

"Please don't contact him." I blurt the words, them catching like poison in my throat at my terror at the idea.

"Oh, I won't, don't you worry." He shakes his head. "I want the old Honor back. I want you to run and fight."

"I can't. I don't feel safe. I can't explain it, but when I had the safeword, I felt as if I could let anything happen because at any point, I could tap out. Do you understand? Now I have no way out. How can I dare to fight you guys off when I have no way at all to stop if it gets too much?"

He strokes his jaw, with the day's worth of dark growth outlining it.

"I do understand. Seeing as, really, we are still playing the game, and you're still going to get the money at the end of the five days, how about you and I make a side deal?"

This is a curveball I wasn't expecting.

"The others need to feel they are getting their vengeance on you for lying. No need for us to share this conversation, but...what about a new safeword? It'll be strictly between you

BRUTAL LIMITS 59

and me, but if you say it, everything stops. Same deal as before. I've put it in fucking writing." He sighs again. "Legally, we really do need it in place. I got...caught up in stuff before. It's not like me. I was pissed. For that, I apologize. However, this place is my baby. I want a new contract signed. Between you and me. Your real name, Honor Armitage, hero cop's stepdaughter. I'll guarantee the money. Two hundred thousand if you tap out. One million if you go the whole way. We both sign. That means I, this place, and the other men are covered, and so are you. As for the others...they don't have to know."

"Why not tell them?" I ask him.

He pauses for a long beat, and when he answers me, the slight color high on his cheekbones tells me he's telling the truth, and it isn't easy for him. "I have a voyeuristic streak, Honor. Not only for watching you...but them. I want to see how they play when they think it is real. It can't be, though. That's not safe. For you or them. Or me. This way, *we* know. But they will be truly primal. They will think this is for real. I've also got a hunch."

"What hunch?"

"That you're going to change everything. And to see if that's true, I need those men to think it's for real."

"Change everything how?"

"Well, that would be giving the game away, wouldn't it?"

I bite at my cuticle, and he slaps my hand away. "Don't make yourself look ratty and ugly. You can have your old room back, too. I'll tell the others it's so you can look pretty for us and smell nice."

I smile in joy. The idea of that old room is amazing.

"But for the old room back, I want the truth, right fucking now. How dangerous is your stepdad?"

"Very. He killed my mom." I don't tell Rafferty what Don wants with me. He might be tempted to give me to him. I know he said the truth, but there's a limit to how far I feel I can go with that after everything that's gone down.

He sucks in a breath. "Fuck."

"Yep." The tears spill over, and I wipe them away with my knuckle.

"You think he's coming after you?"

"I know he is."

"Why?"

Shame fills me, and I don't want to give him all the sordid details. "I know what kind of man he really is, and he doesn't like the idea of there being someone out there who could pull back his mask."

I don't tell Rafferty how, when Don married my mother, he'd had different ideas of what it would be like to have a young, impressionable, teenage girl in the house. Though he never went as far as forcing himself on me, I didn't miss all the 'accidental' touches or the way he always seemed to manage to burst into various rooms when I was in a state of undress.

"And what are the chances of him finding you here?"

I straighten, needing for him to believe me. "He won't," I say with a surety I don't fully believe in. "I've been careful to cover my tracks. As long as you don't register my real name anywhere, he won't track me down."

"I won't use your real name, anyway," he confirms.

I breathe a sigh. It looks like them finding out about Don isn't going to be enough to get me kicked off the island.

But if I think Rafferty is going to be my knight in shining armor, I'm sorely mistaken.

He runs a hand through his hair. "If you can take everything those men out there give, you could leave here a rich woman."

I give a jaded laugh. "Yeah, 'cause God forbid you'd give me the money anyway just to help me."

He shrugs. "Princess, even if I wanted to, I'd have to answer to those three out there, and they wouldn't like me letting you go one little bit. Not one bit. I can't do that to them. This secret deal is enough to make them fucking turn on me if they find out. I want you to have an out, though, if you want it. And, if you take that out," he focuses his deep blue gaze on mine, "you'll still get enough money to get far away from that stepfather of yours. The ball is in your court again, Honor. But I want that fight and spark back."

How do I get it back when I feel so worn down?

Rafferty seems to read my mind.

"First of all, I think a good night's sleep back in your old room and a hot bath, followed by some good food and wine will help. Then tomorrow, we start again." He pauses, and something crosses his features. He speaks again. "Asher's the one you need to be careful with when you're fighting back, but Brody and Wilder? You could take them on hard, and they wouldn't truly hurt you back in return. Don't you want a bit of your power back? Fight them hard, and you can let out some of your anger at the world."

"Do you normally have these conversations with the women at your little resort?"

He laughs, revealing the sort of teeth only top-dollar dentistry can provide. "No, sweetheart. Never. Only you."

"So, why tell me?"

"Two reasons. One, I want you to stay and understand that this time you're signing under your legal name, which means I want you to have full knowledge of where things can go. Two... Like I say, I like to watch. Seeing you, a little, scrappy thing, fighting off Wilder, well, let's just say it gets my motor running."

"Do they know?" I ask. "How much you like watching *them*?"

He grips my face, hard enough to hurt, smooshing my cheeks together. "No. It's no one else's business but mine. You say a word, and you're done here."

I swallow hard. Damn. I keep underestimating this one. Brody, I'm wary of because of his demeanor. Asher, because of my prior experience with him. Wilder, anyone would be wary of because of his size. Rafferty, though. I keep forgetting how terrifyingly cold he can be. The fact he's in control makes it kind of worse.

"I won't say anything," I promise. I mean it, too. I don't want these men fighting one another and absolutely don't want them turning on Rafferty, because in a weird way, he's now my protector in this.

He takes a piece of folded up paper and a small, gold pen out of his back pocket.

"Is that real gold?" I ask.

"Yeah. It was my grandmother's. One of the few things of hers I have left."

"Tell me about your family," I say.

He laughs, a quick, cold bark of a laugh that sounds more like a cough. "No, princess. That's not what I want to talk about."

"Oh, so you get to know all about me, but I can't know about any of you?"

"That's the way this works."

I sigh and rub a hand over my face. These men. These goddamn men. I don't know if I hate them, fear them, want them, or am half falling in love with them.

It might be good for me to really fight back and kick, punch, and scream like a rabid animal because then it will get some of these pent-up emotions out. Hell, maybe I can physically hurt them a little for the way they keep hurting me emotionally.

My size isn't going to be that much of a disparity with a well-aimed kick at their balls, as I proved with Brody.

The new contract is a lot shorter. It doesn't have all the legalese the other one did. "Is this legit?" I ask. "It seems short."

"It is short. Absolutely, it is legit, though. It's simply a lot more basic. See?" He points to the numbered sentences. "It plainly states that we can't kill you or maim you in any way."

"Wow, that's reassuring," I say with heavy irony.

He ignores me completely and carries on. "You can fight back hard, but you can't use any weapons. No sticks or stones." He smirks. "You can run, fight, and hide. You cannot deny us anything sexual, however, once caught. Only by using the safeword can you stop it. Our safeword."

Something comes to me. "What if while I'm running one of them catches me, and you're not there? What if, say, Asher catches me, and he's doing stuff I can't deal with, and I use the word but you're not around?"

Me using Asher as the example is not random.

"Already thought of. It's number four on the list. I'm going to tell them all this evening of some new rules. One of which is none of us can touch you without the others present."

I nod. "But you're not telling them I've signed something new or that I have a safeword?"

He shakes his head. "I'd have put in that caveat about us all being there no matter what. Things seem a little incendiary between you and some of us. Best we only play with all present, going forward."

I read through the other lines, actually making sure I take it all in this time, unlike the first time I signed.

Basically, if I can put up with their depraved shit, I walk off this island a rich woman. And wealth means freedom for me.

The only one who scares me so far as bodily harm goes is Asher. He's a freak with the throat shit, and I can see real moments in his gaze when he looks like he might be about to lose control. The other three scare me more with their insatiable appetites, and their propensity for degradation and casual cruelty.

"Whatever happened to you men to make you this way, you should know, you all need therapy." I sign and hand the sheet back to Rafferty, staring at him angrily.

"*This* is our therapy, princess."

"Clearly not. If it were actual therapy, none of you would be so fucked up anymore."

He laughs and walks to the door. "One last thing, sweetheart. Don't go thinking I will be taking it easy on you because of this little side agreement. I'm still going to expect my pound of delectable flesh from you."

As he opens the door, he pauses and turns back. "*Rainbow*. Don't forget that fucking word. That's your lifeline. You say rainbow, and I stop it all, shove you on the plane, give you the lower amount of money, and drop you off on the mainland. You don't say it? All bets are off, and you're in for a fucking wild time. I'm going to explain to the others that I've agreed you can go back to your room because you're a disgusting stinking mess, and we boys don't like to play with dirty toys. Someone will come for you soon."

He gives me one last long look, a nasty little smirk playing about his pretty mouth, and then he closes the door.

Fucker. He's the biggest fucker of all in some ways, I think. I don't care, though, because he might be a fucker, but he's just thrown me a massive lifeline. I have a safeword again. It makes me feel as if I can deal with anything because I know I have an out. It's the weirdest thing, but psychologically, I honestly think I can do this if I have that out. I'm going to show them. I'll let them have their stupid games, and then at the end of it I will walk away with a fuck ton of their money and my head held high.

Chapter Six
Honor

DESPITE THE NEWLY COMFORTABLE bed, I still tossed and turned during the night, as nightmares besieged me. Still, my sleep was much better than the previous evening.

Sometime after Rafferty left, Brody came for me. He had brought me some clothes but had been sullen and quiet as I dressed. As we walked away from the horror of the bunker toward the resort, he'd held my wrists in a vise-like grip and said nothing.

Marching me to my room, he'd opened the door and practically thrown me in there.

However, once I'd seen the room, his rough treatment of me faded. On the table was enough food to feed five people, never mind one. A bottle of white wine sat chilling and open in an ice bucket. There was cutlery, for God's sake, actual cutlery like a real human being gets, not the way I was treated in that bunker as if I was an animal.

I was so hungry that I'd grabbed a bread roll and stuffed it straight into my mouth. I'd eaten ravenously, and I washed it down with some white wine that I poured myself. Then I decided to have a bath before I ate properly. Most of the food on the table looked like it was already cold. There were cheeses, various sliced meats, bread, and an array of different salads. It was like that Spanish food my mother used to love so much...what was it she called it? Tapas, I think.

The bath had been absolute heaven. The warm water lapped over my aching muscles and cleansed all the dirt of the bunker from my skin. Afterward, I took great care to make sure I wore the scent which Felicity had ordered me to begin wearing on day one of this whole ordeal.

I had washed my hair, dried it straight, and then pulled it up into a ponytail the way I know the men liked. Wearing a simple slip and nothing else, I had eaten my fill of the delicious food, watched some TV—which, thank God, this time wasn't filth but normal programming—and once I began yawning, I padded across the room to the luxurious bedroom and fell onto the soft cloud-like bed.

Of course, now a new day awaits, and I have no idea what sort of depravity will be coming my way.

When I hit my room's dining area, I'm not at all surprised to discover an array of breakfast foods set out for me.

I need my energy today because the games are going to begin again. However, I also don't want a full stomach that will stop me from running. Looking at the food, I decide to go for protein. I take some bacon, with scrambled eggs, and some grilled tomatoes and pile them on to my plate along with just one slice of toast for some energy.

I eat the delicious food, almost moaning every time I take a mouthful, and wash it down with a glass of orange juice and a strong cup of coffee from the carafe steaming in the middle of the table.

Once I've finished eating, I get myself dressed, pulling my hair back up into a ponytail and putting on the tight but easy to run in ensemble that I wear for the games. Then I take my pill.

I apply a minimal amount of makeup, just a tiny bit of bronzer, some mascara, and a dash of lip gloss. I head out of the room, my step light.

I decided something in the middle of the night when I awoke from a particularly bad nightmare.

I'm going to treat this like a job.

The reason I got so hurt and caught up in all of this is because I began to catch feelings for these men. Yet, yesterday, Rafferty showed me that they have no feelings of their own. They can't reciprocate. Even if they wanted to, these men are so messed up that they aren't capable of normal feelings. I simply need to remember that at all times, and keep the money and my future freedom front and center as I play their game. I think the reason most women find this so hard isn't the sexual aspect of it. There's a dark part of me that truly enjoys those games on one level. It's the way they make me feel degraded. But here's the thing about degradation. It can only happen if you let it.

I don't think it will work if I act as if their words and little jibes don't bother me, so I'm going to be an actress. From now on, I'm going to go into these games with my shields up. I'm going to tell myself repeatedly that these men mean nothing to me and whatever they say can't hurt me. For them, however, I'll pretend I'm still bothered by their opinion of me. For some reason, I think that's part of the kick for them. It's all about the power.

I had asked Rafferty yesterday what the hell happened to them to make them this way. I wondered how come four men have such unusual and distinctive tastes, and all happen to be friends with one another. I'm convinced something happened to them all, and it was a shared experience.

Once I'm off this island, I'm going to look into them. I don't know if they're even using their real names, but once I've gotten myself out of the country and I'm in my beautiful villa in Montenegro with my million dollars, I'm going to look these men up. I won't do anything with the information. I don't want any revenge on them. I'm going into this open-eyed and choosing it, after all. However, I am curious. I won't rest until I know why they are the way they are.

I arrive at the same room where I first met them all.

"Today, we're going to play a game of truth, dare, and promise," Rafferty says the moment I enter.

I frown at him. We played a version of this before.

"Only this time it goes something like truth, truth, and more truth. You seem very reticent at telling us anything truthful about yourself." He grins at me, and it's wide and boyish and charming. The man could be a model on television advertising aftershave. "So today, we're going to get you to tell us the truth. I am afraid it means another trip to the bunker."

I automatically take a step back and gasp. "No. I don't want to go back there."

"Don't worry, you won't be sleeping there. However, we do need some of the implements it holds."

Implements? I don't like the sound of that.

"Please, I don't want to. Anywhere but there."

"You don't have any choice, baby girl," Asher says. "I thought you'd figured that out by now."

I do have a choice, but Asher doesn't know that. I have to consciously stop my gaze from flicking to Rafferty. I don't want to give him away.

I lower my head and give a barely perceptible nod.

They walk me back out of the resort and across the island to the bunker, and the whole way there my heart is racing. When we reach it, they open the door, and Wilder turns to me.

"I hope you slept well," he says with a smile. "You're going to need your energy."

Brody gets right in my face. He's still angry. It's written in his stormy gaze.

"Strip, bitch," he orders.

The word *bitch* makes me flinch, but then I remember my promise to myself. This is just a job. I am an actress. I won't take it personally.

I strip methodically and quickly. Once I'm naked, I turn around to find four sets of hungry male eyes staring at me.

"This way," Rafferty says.

He leads me across the floor to where two rings hang out of the ceiling. He takes a key from his back pocket and undoes a set of steel drawers that I had noticed the other day. Out of those, he takes metal handcuffs. He snaps the cuffs closed around my wrists, and I swallow hard.

My arms are dragged over my head and attached to the rings in the ceiling. He slides back what looks like a grate in the floor at each side of my feet and pulls out two more rings. He repeats the process with another set of cuffs from the drawer, but this time big enough to fit around my ankles. My arms are held up and apart, and my ankles are stretched apart so I'm in a starfish position. Naked like this, it makes me feel extremely vulnerable.

"Unlike you," Asher says, "I've not had my breakfast yet."

He kneels in front of me and carefully, and surprisingly gently, parts my folds.

When he starts to lick at me, I think I am going to faint. Oh, my God, the man is talented. He does this thing with his tongue where he swirls it around my clit like he's curling it around a lollipop and then flicks it side to side.

With the other three watching me as if they want to throw Asher off me and fuck me senseless, I can't help but be turned on. I let myself. It's another promise I made. I won't feel guilty for getting turned on by this. It's only natural.

Four incredibly hot men. What woman wouldn't be? It doesn't mean I am a slut or a whore, or all the other words I've been throwing at myself. No, it means I am a healthy young woman with a normal sex drive...Well, almost normal.

The orgasm approaches, and my legs shake. I ride the crest and cry out as... Asher stops.

What the hell?

I gasp and my whole body sags so I'm hanging by my wrists.

"When did your stepfather meet your mother?" Rafferty asks me.

I shake my head, foggy and confused. "Erm, when I was around fifteen," I say.

"Good girl," he says with a rare, genuine smile.

"Do you think he always planned to kill her?" he asks.

I frown. "I don't know. I have no idea. I mean, I don't think so. They seemed happy at first. He acted like the perfect boyfriend."

"Good."

Brody replaces Asher, but he doesn't kneel between my legs. No, he goes and stands behind me. He reaches around my body and holds my pussy lips apart so every single part of me is on display.

"Christ, look at that cunt," Asher says. "Wet, plump, glistening. I'm getting all hungry again."

"I think Wilder deserves a turn," Rafferty says amiably. "With the toy."

Toy?

Wilder smiles and heads to the drawers. He opens one and, unlike the drawer they took the handcuffs out of, the interior is covered in velvet. I spot various toys in there. He takes out a vibrator, small, like a lipstick, and a second dildo that looks scarily big, and heads over to me.

"I love nothing more than seeing tight pussies stretched out. Except normally, I'm the one doing the stretching, so I can't see all that clearly. This time you're going to take this toy. Do you think you can take it, Snow? It's big. It might hurt, but the stretch will help you get ready for more of our cocks."

I nod, my throat dry, heart pounding, but clit pulsing. My nipples are so hard they hurt.

"Keep those pussy lips held open for me," he commands Brody.

Then he applies the small vibrator to my clit, and I almost scream. It's so fucking intense, and my clit is already aching from a denied orgasm.

Wilder gets so close to my clit, I can feel his breath.

"Fucking beautiful," he says in a guttural voice.

"Asher, go and hold the vibrator for him," Rafferty orders. The conductor to their depraved orchestra.

Asher does so, and Wilder gets the big thing and grins at me. "Breathe, Snow."

He places the giant dildo at my entrance. I'm desperate for release, so even though the size is intimidating, I find myself grinding down on it. The head stretches me, and even though there's a burn, that, combined with the vibrator on my clit, feels incredible. Wilder smiles up at me, and I know I've pleased him with my enthusiasm. The thought sends an extra surge of endorphins through me. Why do I want to please these men so much when they're only using me? I know I shouldn't, but I can't help myself.

Wilder pushes the dildo in another inch. I suck in air at first, as it's so big it stretches me tight.

"Oh, God," I cried. "Oh, fuck."

"Out, Snow, breathe *out*. Relax your muscles."

Easy for him to say.

I breathe out, though, and Asher changes the angle of the vibe on my clit, making me yelp as a pulse of intense desire rushes through me. I feel like I'm going to come, and come hard, any second now.

I've got one man holding my lips open so I am pornographically on display for all these men. Another working my clit, and a third pushing a massive dildo into my pussy, all while the fourth watches with the hungriest eyes I've ever seen.

The toy Wilder is using is bent at an angle, and I soon realize why when it hits that spot inside me that these men have discovered.

"Oooh," I moan. It's long and deep, and I don't sound like me.

Wilder presses the toy inside me, not pumping it in and out, but applying pressure and then pulling it away slightly before repeating the motion. I realize he's working my G-spot like a pro, and finally, thank God, I feel a crest of something building again.

A rush of wet seeps out of me, and I cringe in shame, but Asher gathers some on his fingers and sucks them into his mouth.

As I feel the orgasmic contractions start, Wilder pulls the toy out of my pussy so quickly, it's left gripping nothing. Asher stops the toy on my clit and moves it away.

"No!" I practically sob. "Don't stop. Why are you stopping?"

I grind and wriggle my hips and try to squeeze my thighs together, but nothing works. I've still got Brody holding me open, but he's clever about it and makes sure he doesn't brush the sensitive bundle of nerves. The cuffs are holding me in place so I can't touch myself or even close my legs.

Asher swears. "Her clit is fucking *pulsing*, you can see it. Damn, Honor, you're the fucking hottest little bitch we've ever played with."

I don't even have to use my shields now. I'm too turned on by all this to care what they are saying anymore and far too desperate to come to care.

Wilder is still on his knees before me, and he turns his attention to my tits. He cups one in his hand while he covers the other with his mouth. His fingers pinch one of my nipples, and he lightly bites the other. I let out a squeak.

He sucks my nipple harder then lets it pop from between his lips. It's cool down here, and the change in temperature makes it harden even more. I'm breathing heavily and certain I'm going to lose my mind any minute.

"You like that, do you?" he says. "A little pain is sometimes a good thing, right?"

I can't help myself. I nod.

He rises to his feet, and I lift my gaze with him. What's he going to do? The anticipation is almost as bad as being denied my orgasm.

Wilder flattens his palm and gives my left breast a sharp smack. His hard fingers land right on my sensitive nipple, and I jolt at the impact and let out a cry. My skin flares red under his handprint.

He slaps me again, this time on the other tit. I buck, but Brody is still behind me, and the cuffs keep me in place.

"Oh, fuck."

He slaps me again, but this time on my thigh, and then his hand is in front of my pussy, and I know what's coming. I brace myself as his hand lands on my clit and splayed lips. Brody's hand takes some of the impact, but still it vibrates through me like an electric shock.

"Oh, God, please."

I don't even know what I'm begging for anymore. I'm just a needy ball of sensation. All rational thought has left my head. His slaps continue, echoing through the bunker, and instead of cowering from them, I find myself arching my hips forward, wanting his fingers to hit the exact right spot.

Finally, he stops, and he rubs and massages all the places he's slapped, soothing the skin.

"Good girl," he praises me. "You took that so well."

He circles my clit a couple of times, and then his hand falls away.

Another gush of liquid seeps down my thigh, and Rafferty growls and pushes the others out of the way. He's like some male lion about to kill the others to get to a female.

"My turn," he says darkly.

He takes the big toy from Wilder and places it at my entrance once more. He twists it back inside me, groaning when I whimper and more wet seeps out of me.

"That's it, work out that pussy juice like a good little slut," he says.

"I need to come," I moan. God, I sound drunk. My words are slurred and my enunciation all loose as if I've downed a bottle of vodka.

Sex drunk. It must be a thing.

"Were you telling us the truth when you said you didn't intend to deceive us?" he asks, pressing the massive toy against my G-spot and immediately moving it.

"Yes," I scream. I'm sweating, so desperate am I for release.

"Are we in danger from you being here?" Asher demands.

"No. I don't think so. I changed my surname. I've been hiding out. I don't think my stepfather knew where I was. I'd been sleeping on the streets and in cheap motels using only cash when I really needed a bed for the night. I swear, so far as I know, the man doesn't know where I am, and unless any of you tell him, I don't think he will."

"You want to come?" Rafferty asks.

"Yes, please let me come." I am beyond caring that I'm begging.

"You come on a cock not silicone." Rafferty pulls the toy out. "Asher, do you want to do the honors?"

They all laugh, loving their little joke on my name. They've used it before, and it makes me fucking pissed for some reason. I'm so strung out, though, that right now I can't bring myself to say anything. My arms are dead, too, and starting to feel all pins and needles in my hands.

Asher grabs the bedspread and throws it on the floor. "Take her down," he demands.

When my arms are undone, they flop uselessly by my side. Rafferty rubs them, getting the circulation back in my hands for me.

"Get her on the fucking blanket," Asher snarls. "You can do that after."

But Rafferty shakes his head. "No, you can wait. I've decided I want to fuck her mouth first."

I widen my eyes at him, silently begging, but he pushes me to my knees. My legs are already weak, so I offer no resistance.

Rafferty pulls out his cock and grabs my hair. Obediently, I open my mouth, and he slides his cock straight over my tongue. The head hits the back of my throat, and I choke, but he doesn't pull back. His hand tightens in my hair, holding me in place. The musky scent of him fills my nostrils.

He doesn't take things slowly or gently. Just as he'd said he would, he fucks my face, using my mouth and tongue like a sex toy. I gag and choke, and my eyes fill with tears. One trickles down my cheek, and he wipes it away with his thumb and then sucks the salty liquid into his mouth.

He's enjoying my discomfort.

My lips feel swollen and the back of my throat bruised, but he keeps up his rough treatment of me. I close my eyes and draw more air in through my nose.

"Keep your eyes on me, princess," he commands.

I don't dare disobey. I open them again and gaze up at him.

"That's it, pretty liar," he grunts. "You let me fuck your mouth so well."

His cock hardens and swells, and then he comes hard, spilling himself down my throat.

I'm a good girl, and I swallow him down, not spilling a drop.

Rafferty pulls out from between my lips and tucks himself away.

I'm not sure how much more of this I can take.

I'm shaking as Wilder comes forward and lifts me up. He places me on the blanket, and I think he's going to leave me there, but then he lowers his face to my pussy and his tongue circles my clit. I lift my hips to meet him, desperate for more, but he places a kiss to my belly and retreats.

"Needed another taste, Snow."

Asher steps forward. "My turn, and no one is getting in my way this time."

Then, unlike most times I've been with these men, he doesn't merely take his dick out, but he takes all his clothes off. From out of nowhere, he produces a condom, which he tears open and then rolls down his erection.

Asher falls on me. He grabs the base of his cock to position himself at my slit and pushes deep inside in one smooth thrust. He doesn't prepare me, but I don't need it. I let out a grunt at the roughness, but I adjust quickly and am greedy for more. My hips snap up to meet his next thrust as he pounds me into the blanket.

He's almost wild, and I match him. I scratch his back, not even thinking as I dig in deep enough to draw blood, needing it harder, faster, deeper.

"Fuck, yes," he snarls.

Bending his head, he bites my neck where it meets my collarbone. He isn't gentle. Feeling crazed and emboldened, I bite him right back in the same spot, oddly proud when I taste the metallic tang of blood.

A hand wraps around my throat, and panic hits me.

"Hands off her throat," Rafferty orders. "You could have fucked her up the other day. It will still be sore."

Asher growls under his breath but does as Rafferty says.

His thrusts get faster, until he's rutting into me like a dog, and I fall over the edge, my pussy convulsing so hard I sob.

He comes, too, swearing and panting in my ear.

As we slow down and I come back to reality, I'm shocked at how much I lost it.

What the hell was that?

Chapter Seven
Brody

I STARE DOWN AT WHERE Asher is lying between Honor's thighs, both of them breathing hard. My cock is rigid in my jeans, and I'm frustrated and still angry about this whole thing. Can we really believe her about the stepfather not being a danger to us? Is she telling us the truth?

I'm one of those people who struggles to find trust in someone again once I've lost it. I like to think things are black and white. You're either a liar, or you're not, and Honor has already proven she's a liar.

I bring my fingers to my nose and inhale the scent of her cunt from where I'd been touching her.

I need more than that.

"Get off her, Asher," I growl.

He pulls out of her and tosses the used condom to one side. She just lies there, unmoving, dazed. Her legs are open, her pussy swollen and wet and inviting. I still feel like we're treating her too well. Even though her skin is red in places from Wilder's slaps, she's still clearly enjoyed herself.

"Let's hook her back up," I say.

Her gaze snaps to mine, her eyes widening. "What?"

"I wasn't talking to you."

Rafferty arches a dark brow at me, clearly wondering what I've got planned.

Wilder bends down and hauls her back up by her arms.

She shakes her head. "I need to rest."

"You rest when we say you rest," he growls.

She sucks in a shaky breath, and he clips her wrists back inside the cuffs. I move up behind her again.

"Hello, Pan," I say against the back of her ear. "Ready for round two?"

She doesn't reply, but just hangs from the rings in the ceiling.

I look to Asher. "Where's that vibrator?"

He picks it up from where he'd left it on the top of the cabinet and hands it to me.

"I'm going to need lube as well," I say.

He grins and tosses me a tube."

Honor lifts her head. "Wha—what are you going to do to me?"

I click open the top of the lube bottle and place it at the top of the crease of her bottom. I squeeze a good dollop of it onto her skin and watch as the heat from her body turns it from gel to liquid and it slides down between the twin globes of her ass.

"Guess," I say.

"Oh."

I think she gets the idea. The lube is trickling down over her asshole now, and I flick on the small vibrator. A buzzing fills the room.

The vibrator is small, and I don't want to risk losing my grip on it. I part her cheeks with one hand and then run the vibrator

BRUTAL LIMITS 83

down her crease, to land on her tight star. She bucks and gives a sexy little moan. I experiment, running the toy around her ring, and then pushing it inside her just a fraction of an inch. She squirms and pulls down on the cuffs attaching her arms to the ceiling.

With my other hand, I flick open the buckle of my jeans and then pop the button and drag down the zipper. I reach in and pull myself out, then surround my cock with my fist. I feel like I've been hard for hours, and my eyes roll with pleasure at those first few pumps. I want to keep them open, though, especially since I have this hot piece of ass hanging from the ceiling and I'm currently teasing her asshole with a vibrator.

This is too good to miss.

Precum leaks from my slit, and I take the vibrator away for a moment and rub the fluid onto her asshole.

She lets out a whimper, and I get even harder.

"I'm clean," I tell her, "and I'm fucking your ass bare. Got it? I'm going to come inside you and fill you up so it's going to still be dripping out of you for hours to come."

She's no anal virgin. Asher took her this way just a couple of days ago, and I'm sure the others will all want their turns over the days to come. I'm doing her a favor, really, getting her prepared for what's in store.

Maybe I should be more gentle with her, but I'm still angry about her lies and I take my anger out on her. She's all nicely lubed up, and even though the vibrator hasn't gone any way in stretching her asshole, I know her previous orgasm will have softened those muscles. I place the head of my cock against her tight little hole and thrust my hips forward.

Honor lets out a cry, but I don't stop.

Her asshole opens up around me beautifully, the tight walls hugging my cock head.

"Fuck, that feels good."

I ram myself deeper, deliberately not being gentle with her. She cries out again, and I grab both her tits to hold her in place.

"Oh, that stings."

"Just relax, Pan."

The others look on, but no one says anything. Inch after inch of my dick slides inside her body, and I stare down at where her asshole is stretched around me.

I smack her ass cheek and make it jiggle. "Such a perfect little peach of a bottom. All ripe for the taking."

I slide balls deep and hold myself still for a few seconds, before pulling out a couple of inches. Then I ram back inside her, and her whole body jerks, her tits bouncing. She gasps. Fuck, that's hot. My groin is a knot of heat and tension, and I want to find my release, but I want to put her through it first.

She's not getting away so easily.

I look over her shoulder at one of the others in particular. "I think her pussy needs filling. What do you say, Wilder?"

She stiffens, and her ass tightens around my dick. Oh, yes, this is going to be fun.

"What? Both of you?" she says.

"Abso-fucking-lutely."

She shakes her head. "No, I can't. This is too much."

"It's too much when we say it's too much."

Wilder approaches, his hand already at his zipper. He opens his pants and pulls out his huge cock. It's bigger than the dildo we've just used on her, and the metallic glint of his piercing catches in the light. I can't see her face from where I'm standing, but I can imagine her expression and the way her gaze is most likely locked on his monster dick.

Wilder masturbates for a moment, running his hand up and down his length. He pauses at the tip to lightly flick at the piercing, and I can't help but wonder what it feels like. I wonder how it will feel for Honor, too. I'm sure it'll be good, once her body adjusts to being so full.

He moves closer, crowding into her personal space. He catches her by the chin and kisses her, long and slow and deep. From the way her entire body relaxes, I can tell it's the right thing to do. I hold still, fighting my instinct to just rut into her like an animal.

Wilder bends his knees to position himself at her pussy.

She freezes, though she still has my dick in her ass. "No, please. I don't think I can."

"Just the tip, Snow," he tells her. "Take that, and we'll go from there."

She stares at him. "I really don't think I can."

"You can and you will."

"No, no, please, I can't."

I'm aware she no longer has her safeword. I exchange a glance with Wilder, and I can tell by the seriousness of his eyes that he's thinking the same as me. I reach around and catch her chin in my fingers and twist her face so she can look at me. The position is awkward, but I want her to be looking at me so I can read the truth on her face.

"Do you want us to stop, Honor? Do you *really* want us to stop? Because we will, right now, if that's really want you want."

She takes a sip of air, her chest rising and falling. Her eyes slip shut for the briefest of seconds and then open again. When she speaks, it's not far from a whisper.

"No, I don't want you to stop."

A smile touches my lips. "Good girl."

Wilder grabs her thigh and hooks it around his hip, opening her up to him. I have to shift my position slightly to accommodate him. I know this is going to feel intense, how tight and crowded it'll be inside her, with me competing for space with Wilder. That's not a bad thing, though.

She moans as he presses inside her—just the tip, as he'd promised. I can feel the change in pressure against my cock, and I know it's only going to get more powerful.

He shunts inside her a little more.

"Give me some of that lube," he says to me.

He uses a healthy dollop, rubbing it all around his cock and over her pussy. When he plays with her clit, her ass contracts and releases around me. I have to close my eyes and drop my head to her damp, sweaty shoulder to hold myself together.

Wilder slides in a little more.

Honor is panting. She leans into me, so I'm half holding her up. A moment ago, I was the bad guy, but now she's needing me for support. I try not to experience the warmth inside me at the thought, and fail.

Fuck.

"I'm halfway in now, Snow," Wilder says. "Almost there."

"Oh, God. Oh, fuck."

The way she squirms makes me even harder. I don't want to come yet. I need a bit of time with us both moving inside her, but she's coated in sweat and naked and wriggling between us. Having Wilder's cock inside her as well means the pressure around my dick is enough to make me lose my mind.

"You did it, Snow," Wilder says. "You did so well. I'm right inside you. Look."

He creates a little space between them so she can peer down and see where her pussy is stretched around his huge girth.

"Oh, God," she says. "I think I'm going to pass out."

Wilder smirks. "Not yet, you won't. Wait until you come."

I meet his eyes again, and he gives me an almost imperceptible nod. It's his way of telling me he's ready.

I reach to the front of her body again to rub her clit. Honor moans, and this time she's the one who initiates the movement. Her hips arch, back and forth, pushing deeper on me, while pulling off of Wilder's cock, and then moving forward again. We find a rhythm, slow and careful at first, then getting fiercer with every thrust. Our hands and mouths are all over her, her head is flung back, her lips parted. The noises she's making barely sound human, and I realize we've taken her to her basest of states. Her body is a mere toy between us—holes to fuck, breasts to suck, a mouth to claim—and she doesn't seem to care.

The pleasure inside me mounts higher and higher still. I slam into her ass, no longer caring if I'm hurting her. My balls are high and tight in my body, and it's only going to be seconds before I keep my promise of filling her ass with my cum. I keep up the rhythm of my fingers on her clit. Wilder's face is a tense picture of concentration.

"Oh, fuck, oh, fuck. I'm coming," Honor cries.

Her entire body goes rigid between us, and the sound she lets out is guttural and raw. Her pussy and ass convulse around our cocks, and I know I'm not going to last another second.

I give in to my orgasm and jam myself deep in her ass as I spill my cum inside her. My cock jerks and my balls contract, releasing stream after stream.

Wilder somehow manages to hold on, and he pulls out of her and releases his cum all over her belly. It wasn't until that moment that I realize he'd been fucking her bare, too. That was hell of a risk to take.

Honor slumps between us, all the energy gone out of her. She's hanging from her wrists, but she's using me as support so her arms aren't taking the weight. I kiss her shoulder, her skin hot and damp, and put out my hand for one of the others to pass me the keys for the cuffs. Rafferty does so, and I undo her from them, then hold her against me as she slumps down.

Wilder blows out a breath and shoves his long, wavy hair away from his face. "Fuck, that was intense."

"You can say that again." I look to Honor. "You okay, Pan?"

She doesn't speak, but nods.

I glance to the others. "She's done for the day. She gets to go back to her room now."

She tenses in my arms. "The room at the resort?"

"Yeah. I think you've earned it."

She relaxes again and empties all the air from her lungs.

I check my emotions. I went into this angry with her, but with my climax, some of that anger has melted away. I still haven't fully forgiven her for lying to us, but maybe I will, one day.

Chapter Eight
Honor

I'M SO EXHAUSTED I can barely think straight.

I've never had an orgasm like that before—where I'm literally frightened I might lose my mind. I'm relieved I don't have to stay in the bunker, however, and I get to go back to my room.

Brody carries me across the island, toward the resort. His cum is trickling out of me, and I know I should be embarrassed, but it was what he wanted. I have my arms around his neck and my head on his shoulder, and the gentle pace of his walking lulls me into a doze. I hope I've done enough to please the men.

We reach the resort, and Brody carries me back to my room, the others following.

I hope they don't plan another epic sex session. There is no way my body can handle anything more. I already know I'm going to be tender and bruised after taking both Wilder and Brody at the same time. I can hardly believe I've done it, and some silly part of me actually feels proud of myself.

I push away those nagging little voices that try to tell me I'm a slut and a whore for letting them do whatever they want to me. Yes, maybe I'm here for the money and safety of the island—and the safety of having the four of them around me—but I also enjoyed it, and there's nothing wrong with that.

I wonder what would happen if my stepfather did turn up here. Would the guys hand me over to him, or would they protect me as though I was truly theirs?

"Let's run her a bath," Rafferty says. "She earned it."

Asher goes to the phone. "I'll order some food."

The rush of water hitting the porcelain of the tub reaches my ears, followed by the sweet aroma of the signature scent they like me to use. Brody takes me into the bathroom, and steam dampens my skin.

When the bath is almost full, he carefully lowers me into the water. I sigh with pleasure, and my eyes slip shut.

This is my happy place, I realize. Here, I am completely relaxed and at peace.

I think of all the nights I spent out on the street, how I would have given anything for even a clean sink to wash myself. Now I'm in the lap of luxury, and all I had to sell was my body.

The men surround me, getting to their knees so they can reach me in the tub. I suck in a breath, worrying that they're going to want more sex, but instead, they pour soap onto sponges or into their palms and wash me.

There's nothing sexual in it. They soap down my limbs and wash my hair. Wilder's strong fingers massage my scalp, and I groan with pleasure. Even when Asher washes my breasts, I feel nothing but tenderness in his touch.

A knock comes at the door.

"Room service," Wilder says and goes to answer the door. He calls out from the adjoining room, "You have a choice of champagne or a good malbec, filet steak with potatoes, and a chocolate torte for dessert."

It sounds incredible, and my stomach gurgles with hunger. I can't help hoping that the bath and food mean they've forgiven me for my lies. I don't want to get too cocky, though. They can pull the rug out from under my feet whenever they want.

"We'll leave you to soak," Rafferty says. "You'll need to regain your energy for what comes next."

It's on the tip of my tongue to ask him exactly what will come next, but I decide I'd rather not know. It's easier to deal with things as they're happening rather than worry about them until tomorrow.

Chapter Nine
Rafferty

IT'S BEEN SEVERAL HOURS since we left Honor in the tub, and I've gone to the office to finalize some paperwork. I discover I'm not in there alone.

"What are you doing?" I ask.

Asher is hunched over his laptop—as per usual—but there is a new kind of intensity about him.

"Just looking for someone," he replies, without glancing over at me.

"Pastor Wren?" I check.

We last heard of him being in Reno, and it hasn't escaped my thoughts that we haven't done anything about it yet. We need to know his exact location and order our private investigator to note down Wren's routine. Before we do anything, we have to know precisely where he's going to be and when. We'll only get one chance at this, and we can't take the risk of fucking it up. Right now, the element of surprise is on our side. Wren has no idea his past victims are stalking him, but, if he gets wind of it, he'll be gone. He's already changed his name multiple times, has shut down, and re-opened churches in different locations to stay ahead of anyone figuring out what a sick son-of-a-bitch he really is. When the time comes for us to grab him, we don't want there being any chance of the police tracking either us or him down again. We all plan to take our time—to make him suffer, like he made us suffer.

Asher doesn't reply, but his fingers continue to fly across the keyboard, the faint clicking of the keys audible.

"Well?" I prompt.

I don't appreciate people not answering me.

Asher sighs and sits back. "It occurred to me that if we're so concerned about Honor's stepfather trying to find her and locating her here, why don't we just make sure we find him first? If we know where he is, then we won't get any surprises."

So, his mind isn't on Pastor Wren either. I wonder who he's really doing this for.

"*We* won't get any surprises?"

He shrugs. "And neither will she."

"She's only here for a few more days, and then she gets to leave a rich woman."

"Maybe," he says.

I frown. "What do you mean by maybe?"

"We don't know that she'll want to leave."

I chuckle at that. "You have seen what we've put her through, right? I'd say it's a safe bet that she'll want to leave at the end of this."

He purses his lips. "What if we don't let her?"

I pause, letting the implication of what he's just suggested sink in. I wonder if he's finally lost his mind.

I speak firmly, but my tone is cool. "Ash, if we don't let her leave at all, that's false imprisonment. At the level that you're suggesting, it's considered a felony."

"Maybe."

"No," I say, even firmer this time. "It's not a maybe. What you're suggesting could get us in a whole heap of shit. You really want to spend time behind bars? And what about her, huh? What about Honor? She is a human being, no matter how we've treated her. Once this is done, she gets to live her life with a million bucks in her pocket."

He bites his lower lip. "And never sees any of us again."

"Exactly."

My chest tightens at the thought. Is that why Asher is getting all uptight—because he feels the same way?

A muscle in Asher's jaw ticks. "This will be over for us then. You understand that, don't you? Once she's gone, no other girl is going to come close. They'll all be pale imitations."

"You don't know that."

I'm arguing with him, but I can't help feeling he's right.

How are we supposed to bring any more women here once Honor has gone? I think back to all the ones who'd come before her. They were fun and everything, but none even held a candle to her. Now I think back, I realize just how fake it had always felt before. Sure, they'd run from us, and had kicked and screamed and even clawed us when we'd caught them. They'd told us to stop and cried out 'no' when we hadn't, but we'd always known it was just a game.

A game.

That's the difference with them compared to Honor. With her, it doesn't feel like we need to pretend. Even though she's lied, nothing about her feels fake.

"I do," Asher says simply. "And you do, too. This side of things will be over once she's gone."

I need to change the subject. I'm worried about where Asher's mental state will deteriorate to if he truly believes this side of our lives will be over without Honor. Should I put him first? He's more than a friend—he's like a brother to me—and surely he should mean more to me than some girl we've known barely a week. He does—of course he does—but we still can't break the law. How badly would Asher's mental health deteriorate if we were in prison?

Something else occurs to me. If we end up behind bars, then we can never finish what we'd started with Pastor Wren.

"Tell me what you've found out about the stepfather," I say instead.

"Not much, so far, but I've only just started looking. He's based at the Los Angeles Police Department in West LA. I've got a phone number for the station."

I frown at him. "What are you going to do? Call up and ask for him by name?"

Asher shrugs. "Why not?"

"He's going to want to know who you are."

"I won't say anything. This number is untraceable."

I don't understand. "If you don't want to talk to him, what's the point in phoning?"

"If he's at the police station in Los Angeles, then he's nowhere near Honor."

I like his thinking. "Good point." Something else occurs to me. "Unless he's paid someone else to track her down. He's a police officer. I bet he has contacts."

"Let's find out if he's there first."

Asher uses his laptop to make the call. I assume he has some kind of VPN on it that'll prevent the location being traced.

Computers aren't my thing, but I trust Asher knows what he's doing.

It rings for a painfully long time, and I wonder if anyone is even going to pick up.

"Good thing this isn't an emergency," I mutter, but then realize that if it was, we'd have called nine-one-one and not the direct number for the station.

Finally, someone answers. "LAPD." A feminine voice, bored sounding, drifts out of the laptop. "How can I help you?"

Asher puts on his most formal tone. "I need to speak with Detective Don Bowen as a matter of urgency."

"One minute, please."

We're put on hold, and tinny music plays over the computer speakers.

The female voice returns, and the music stops. "Sorry to keep you waiting."

"Don't worry. I was enjoying the tunes."

He winks at me, and I roll my eyes.

"Umm, right. I'm afraid Detective Bowen is on vacation right now. Can I take a message or redirect your call to another detective?"

Asher doesn't bother saying anything else. He just ends the call and slowly spins in his chair to face me.

"Vacation," I say. "You should have asked how long he's been gone and when he's expected back."

"Why? What would that tell us? We already know he isn't there."

There'd been no point in asking where Detective Bowen had gone. It's not as though they would have told us.

I twist my lips. "He could be anywhere."

"Somewhere nearby," Asher suggests.

I don't like the idea of that, and for some reason, it makes me defensive.

"Yeah, he could be, but I'll tell you one place he's not, and that's right here. He's not getting on the island. We have cameras all over this place and we'd know if anyone was here who shouldn't be. Honor is perfectly safe at the resort. That asshole of a stepfather isn't coming anywhere near her."

"Why are you so worried about her?" Asher eyes me curiously.

"I'm not. I'm just protecting my business."

He snorts. "Yeah, right."

"You were the one looking up her stepfather," I shoot back accusingly.

He folds his arms and smirks. "To protect the business."

We both know that isn't the case. Hell, a moment ago, he was talking about making her stay forever, for fuck's sake. Since neither of us wants to admit it out loud, I don't push it.

I blow out a breath. "Okay, so if we know he's not at work, how do we find him?"

"I'll do a search on bank and phone records. If I can find out who he uses, I can hack their systems. If he's placed a call recently or used a credit card, I'll be able to pinpoint his most recent location. If he's sunning himself on a beach in Mexico, we won't need to worry."

"How long is that going to take?"

"It's not really something I can answer. Could take a few hours. Could take days."

Fuck. I don't want it to be days.

"We should tell the others," I say. "We all need to be on the same page."

Asher nods. "You're the boss."

We find Wilder and Brody in the cinema room. They haven't chosen what they're going to watch yet, but have loaded themselves up with snacks—buckets of salted popcorn and trays of nachos. They clearly worked up an appetite after the time spent with Honor, though right now they seem more intent on throwing the popcorn at each other than eating it.

Brody catches sight of my face. "Uh-oh. What's happened."

I fill them in on what we've just learned.

Brody's expression darkens. "Why the fuck are we wasting time on Honor's stepfather? This is nothing but a distraction from what we're supposed to be focused on—pinning down that son of a bitch, Wren."

"I get that," I say, "but this is important, too."

"Nothing is more important than finding Wren. He could still be up to his perverted ways, for all we know, and every day spent worrying about some cop who has nothing to do with us is just another day wasted."

Asher shrugs. "Aren't we wasting days, anyway. I mean, chasing Honor around the island is hardly focusing."

"We need that," Brody growls. "We all do. If we don't have that release, we'll all end up losing our shit."

Wilder agrees. "We deserve to still get to have a life. Just because he stole our childhoods from us doesn't mean he gets to steal the rest of our lives as well."

I need to rein this back in. Emotions are running high, and people aren't thinking clearly.

"Slow down. No one is saying we take our eye off the ball with Wren. All we're saying is we have something else to consider now as well. Honor said she's running from her stepfather, and right now, we don't know where that stepfather is. We can't pretend that isn't a concern for us."

"Why is it a concern for us?" says Brody. "We throw her off the island and be done with it. It's not our business."

I arch an eyebrow at him. "Is that really what you want?"

I already know it isn't. Brody's acting all tough because we didn't listen to him when Honor first came to the island, and I know he's still pissed at that. Wilder's still pissed cause she'd lied, and I think he was the one who'd been falling for her the hardest. Asher is...well, just Asher. He doesn't fall for anyone. As for me, I don't want anyone bringing their shit to the resort, but I feel like that ship has already sailed. Now it's my job to manage the fallout without any more damage.

"If we dump her back on the mainland, even with the money, he might still track her down," Wilder says.

Brody purses his lips. "So what if he does? That isn't our concern."

His comments still surprise me. "Really? You're that hard-hearted? She believes he killed her mother, and from the fear I see in her eyes when she talks about him, I'm guessing she thinks he'll do the same to her to keep her quiet. Don't tell me that you're fine with that."

"This isn't our problem," Brody mutters again.

I consider Brody's suggestion of just getting her off the island. I don't like it, but wouldn't that be the most sensible thing to do?

My emotions war inside me. For one, I've signed a new contract with her now—one the others don't know about—and if I throw her off the island, I'll be the one breaking it. Asher's words about how this side of things will be over for us after she leaves also ring in my ears.

Maybe I just don't want to let her go either.

Chapter Ten
Honor

DESPITE THE FOOD AND the comfort of the bath, I find myself feeling increasingly low as the evening progresses. I'm in the nice room again, and the luxury is wonderful. However, I'm lonely. The guys all have each other, and I have no one. Even if they did let me join them, which is very doubtful, I'd be the odd one out. The punchline at the end of the joke. The toy they like to use and then put back in its box.

I wish there was someone I could talk to, even if only briefly.

Bored, as well as down, I flick through the TV channels, sighing when I find nothing worth watching.

Pushing myself up from the sofa, I stand and pace the room. Perhaps I ought to go for a walk? Would I even be allowed to now? After what I've done, it might be best to stay in my room. I don't want to make the men suspicious of me again, even if I am just taking an innocent walk. Today's games were purely sexual, and didn't include any chase, so I actually have some pent-up energy within me. I'm both boneless and languid from the sex, but at the same time oddly restless.

Blowing out a long breath, I walk to the window and look out. It's dark outside, so I can't see much, but leaves move in the breeze, and the strangest sense of desolation washes over me.

Loneliness is an awful feeling. And I have been lonely for a long time. You can be in a house full of other people, and if those people mistreat you, or deride you, then you can still feel completely and utterly alone.

That's how I felt most of the time during the last couple of years of Mom's life. She was so swept up in Don that I swear she didn't see me anymore. Then, of course, I captured his creepy attentions. I spent so many nights just shut up in my room that those four walls became my prison.

Perhaps I ought to go for a swim? Burn off some energy. Then again, I've had a bath and styled my hair the way that *they* like it, and I've also eaten quite a lot of food. Mom used to tell me when I was small that if you went swimming after eating a lot of food, you could drown. I'm pretty sure that's an urban myth, but it's still best not to risk it.

The door to my room opens, and Asher strolls in as if he owns the place, which in fact he kind of does.

"Are you okay?" he asks.

"I suppose so," I say, though his question surprises me. He doesn't often seem to care much for my wellbeing.

"What kind of answer is that?" He shakes his head at me. "What the fuck is wrong with you?"

He asks the question as if me not being one hundred percent cheery and happy is a personal affront to him.

God, why does he always have to be so abrasive? I shrug, raising my arms and letting them fall back down again, slapping against my thighs.

"Do you want to come and join us? Maybe watch a movie?" he asks.

He chews his lip as his eyes dart around the room. I can almost hear him screaming inside, *please say no*.

He is so uncomfortable asking me the question I almost laugh. It's clear that Asher is not used to being around women at all, unless they service in him in some way or another.

"I'd rather not, if that's okay. I'm not in a movie mood," I reply truthfully. "I'm just feeling lonely. I miss my best friend. She's literally my only friend in the world, which I guess makes me truly pathetic. And normally I speak to her pretty regularly."

He watches me for a long moment, then scratches his cheek. "I could configure the laptop and find a way for you to speak to her which wouldn't give away your location, if you want?"

My jaw drops. It's never occurred to me that any of the men might offer me contact with people outside of the resort.

"Oh, my God, really? You can do that?" I jump up and down on the spot twice, and then get hold of myself because I realize I'm behaving like a big kid.

For once in his life, the man observing me doesn't say anything nasty, or even give that knowing smirk of his. Instead, he just smiles. His smile is so genuine and carefree, it's like a punch to the gut.

God, when he smiles this way, Asher is beautiful.

For a moment, I get an image of how he might have been as a little boy before whatever happened to him corrupted his soul.

"Really," he tells me. "But there are rules. You can't say anything that will give away where you are. Remember you signed a non-disclosure agreement, and it's legally binding. Anyway, I doubt you want your stepfather finding you, no?"

He doesn't need to use my stepfather as a threat. There is absolutely no way I want that man finding me.

"I won't say a word, I promise. I'll simply tell her that I found a motel to stay in for a night or two and managed to grab the chance to give her a call. She doesn't know I'm on the run from my stepfather, so I wouldn't tell her the truth, anyway."

He watches me warily for a long moment, and I see the second he makes his decision. He stands little straighter and gives a brief nod.

"All right, then. I'll need to check with Rafferty first, and make sure he's okay with this, but I can't see him having an issue with it. You say anything, any fucking thing that gives us away, and you'll wish you'd never been born. In fact—" he takes three rapid steps toward me, his face menacing, "—you give this operation away in any shape or form, and you'll wish that your stepfather had found you, trust me."

Then he turns smartly on his heel and stalks out of the door, shutting it with a slam behind him.

He is the most mercurial man I have ever met. One moment he's almost nice, and the next he's a complete dick.

Still, if he gives me the chance to speak to my friend, I think I can forgive him almost anything.

After what seems like forever, the door opens again and Asher storms in. He's got an expensive-looking laptop bag slung over his shoulder.

For someone who looks so harmless at first glance, you soon realize that out of all the four men, Asher is the force of nature among them in many ways. I can imagine he's the sort of person who, if he wants to know something, simply won't let it go. He'll keep searching and searching until he finds that nugget of information he wants, no matter what. If he decides he's done with you, he will be done. No guilt. No worries.

Yeah, he's not one to be messed with, and I made the mistake of thinking he was the nicest at first. More fool me.

He opens a laptop and places it on the table. Then he takes out a phone and connects it to the laptop with a cable before messing around and doing something that looks ridiculously complicated.

My heart leaps with hope, and my pulse picks up pace in anticipation of getting to talk to someone who's actually on my side for once.

"If you give me her number, I'll call it for you now." He waves the phone at me as if to emphasize his words.

I reel off Ruth's number, which I know by heart.

He drops the number into the phone keypad, but before he presses the button to call, he pauses and turns to me.

"I'm going to trust you and give you some privacy right now. If, however, you say anything to give information to your friend, or look at anything else on this phone once you've hung up the call, or indeed the laptop, then I'm done with you. I think you know by now what I'm capable of if I'm done with somebody for good."

His words are so eerily echoing of my thoughts earlier, they send a chill right down my spine.

"I swear to you, I won't do anything other than speak to Ruth, and my conversation will be as vague as can be when it comes to where I am and what I'm doing."

"Okay, then, you're good to go."

He presses the call button and hands me the phone before he leaves the room.

The phone rings out five, six, and then seven times. My heart sinks as Ruth doesn't answer. Damn. She's probably out somewhere, partying it up. Just as I'm about to hang up, a familiar voice echoes down the phone at me.

"Hello?" she asks, somewhat unsure.

"Ruth? It's me, Honor."

"Honor? Oh, my God."

She squeals so loudly I have to hold the phone away from my ear or I'll go deaf.

"What the hell, bitch? Where have you been? I've been worried sick about you. Everybody's worried about you."

"What do you mean, everybody? Everybody, who?"

"Just people." She gives a laugh. "You know what it's like round here. Everyone keeps saying 'where's Honor, have you seen Honor, where is she?' Nosy fuckers. Of course, your stepfather is generally worried sick about you. You said a short break when you texted me. It's been a while."

The mere mention of Don has my joy turning to icy dread.

Ruth continues. "He asked about you only the other day."

"What do you mean?" I ask.

"Don," she says as if I've forgotten the name of my stepfather and who he actually is.

"What has he been saying?" I clarify.

I realize I must sound really pissy, because when she speaks next, it is with a hurt tone to her voice.

"He just asked if I'd heard from you. I thought it was strange what with you just being away and all. He seems to think that there's something more going on. He says you're in trouble, Honor. Is that true? You know you can tell me anything and it will go to the grave."

I do know that. Ruth is a trustworthy person. The trouble is my stepfather is vicious and ruthless, and he would stop at nothing to get the information out of her.

I've also made a promise to Asher, and no matter how I might feel about the man, which right now is both grateful and also livid because of the way he talks to me, I won't betray his trust again.

"I really am okay," I tell her. "I just needed to get away after Mom, you know? I didn't tell Don everything because he's being kind of..." I wrack my brains to think of something I can say that won't give away anything to do with my stepfather. Not the truth, but something to give me a good enough reason not to have told him exactly what's going on. "I suppose you could say that since Mom's died, he's been overbearing. And I get that he worries about me and cares about me as if he were my own father, but it can be a bit much." The words almost choke me, they're so untrue. The truth, though, will put Ruth in danger, too. "I just felt like I needed a bit of privacy and a bit of time to myself, without going into all the reasons with him. He'd only have tried to stop me leaving."

"Well, if you're sure, babe." She doesn't sound like she believes me.

"Anyway, I haven't got long because I had to wrangle a phone to call you on. I was an idiot and managed to drop mine, and the screen is fucked. It's costing me a small fortune to fix, but I'm working on it."

"Give me the number you're calling me on," she exclaims. "It didn't come up when you called me. Then I'll call you back."

I have to think quickly. "Oh, I can't. It's a shared number and there's a rule about handing it out, sorry." I change the topic. "So, enough about me. I want to know what's going on with you."

"Okaaaay."

I can tell that she's unsure about this and she thinks there's more to my story, but then she sucks in a breath and starts to talk to me at a hundred miles an hour. Pure Ruth as she rattles words out machine gun style. I smile as I realize she's missed me as much as I've missed her.

"You won't believe what's happened," she says excitedly. "You know Davey, the boy I like? The one from the coffee shop. Well, he asked me out!"

"He did not?" I exclaim.

"Girl, he did."

"You need to tell me all about it, starting right from the beginning," I say.

"I'd gone into the coffee shop when it was almost closing time, and there was literally no one else in there." She gives a short laugh. "I mean, normally it's full of people at that time, right? You know, all the kids hanging out after school, and our little gang that would go and sit and get coffees and cakes before we got thrown out because they were closing up. Well, there was no one there this night at all. So anyway, I went in, grabbed a coffee, and I said to him like, 'Just make it to go because you're closing.' I didn't wanna put him out. He says to me, 'Oh, it's fine. I've got lots of work left to do. You can eat and drink them here, if you want.' So of course, I say okay, and that's great, and thank you, all the polite stuff. All the time, though, I'm thinking, yeah this gives me more time to watch him as he goes around clearing up and bussing the tables. You know how I like to watch his ass, right?"

She cracks up at herself, and I join in, feeling transported right back home. It's as if I'm in the bedroom with her, sipping a Coke and just chatting with my bestie.

"Go on, then, tell me more," I push.

"Well, there I am, sipping at my coffee and trying to casually eye-fuck him without him realizing what I'm doing."

"I think you mean casually objectify him, don't you?" I say with a giggle. "Surely, eye-fucking is something that is done openly."

"Okay, my bad. You get what I mean, though. So, anyway, he's going around wiping the tables, putting everything away, and I'm just thinking, *Oh my God, he is so hot*. And then he comes over to me and I'm ready for him to tell me I have to go now because he's going to lock the door. Instead, he takes a seat opposite me, and then he just folds his hands under his chin and looks at me."

"Just looks at you?" I ask. "In what way? Like, a sexy way, or was it weird? Or maybe kind of dark and brooding."

"Definitely dark and brooding, with quite a lot of hot 'n' sexy on the side. Honestly, he looked like he wanted to eat me alive. I was like, where is this coming from? I always thought I just had a completely one-sided crush on the guy. Then he says... and get this...he says, 'Are we going to stop screwing around and do this or what? You like me, and I like you, so why don't we go and grab a drink?'"

"Wow." I'm impressed, his lines are good.

I'd always taken him as being a bit of a beta boy, and that's great because after my time on this island with these four alphas, I think my next relationship is going to be beta all the way. This behavior is full on alpha dude, though.

"So, what did you say?"

"Obviously, I said yes, and I'm going to go. He wants me to meet him at a place downtown in two nights, and we're going to get a drink and hang out and watch a band."

"That's amazing, babe. I'm really happy for you."

"So, what about you? Where are you right now? Any hot guys?"

For a crazy moment, I want to say, 'Yeah four of them, and they stuff me full of their dicks every day, in every way.'

I don't.

Asher said I couldn't tell her where I was, but he didn't say that I couldn't answer any questions about it at all. I need to say something, or it's going to seem weird. So even though it breaks my heart, I take in a deep breath, blow it out and lie to my best friend. "You're not going to believe me if I tell you. I'm in Portland."

"Portland?" she exclaims.

"Yeah." I laugh.

There's a café in San Francisco that we loved to go to whenever we visited the city, that has a sign above the door, saying 'We're just itching to get away from Portland.' We used to wonder what was so bad about it.

"You went to Portland?" she squeals. "What's it like?"

"Kinda cool." I wrack my brains and try to retrieve what little I know about Portland. "It's kind of a hippy place, you know, it's got that vibe. I suppose maybe a bit like San Francisco but a lot cleaner. I don't know... it's hard to describe. It's green." I recall an article about how Portland was supposed to be the greenest city in America. I'm warming to my theme a bit now because if she does give in and tell Don something, it's good if he thinks I'm in Portland and spends time looking there. "There's a lot of bikes that you can hire and pedal around on, and lots of green this and green that. Places to fill up your car with electricity and not gas, you get the idea."

"Do you think you'll stay there long?"

"Maybe, I'm not sure. But listen, babe, I have to go in a minute, but I promise I'll call again as soon as I can. It's been so good to hear your voice. And I need you to send me pics of the outfit you choose for your date."

As soon as I say it, I realize I've made a mistake. I won't be able to see the pictures and I won't be able to reply, which may make her suspicious.

Then it hits me. By it by the time she goes on her date, I'll only have a couple of days left on this island. I can reply a few days late, apologize, and have a long chat with her. At that point, I might be in Montenegro and truly free.

The thought should have me all happy and excited, but instead I get a sinking feeling in the pit of my stomach.

Even if I can manage to go the whole hog and complete the last few days and leave here with the whole amount of money, I'm still going to be alone again. I'm still going to be out there and vulnerable. Will even a million dollars be enough to stop Don?

"Okay, babe, I will, but fix your damn phone so you can reply. I need your help. I need to know what outfit is best. I'll take pictures of a few and send them your way. You tell me which one to go for. I'm thinking like sexy, but not slutty. I'll save that for date three. So, sexy, but kind of highbrow sexy, you know what I mean? Like a librarian, on a date."

"Ruth, you don't want to go for the librarian on a date vibe, trust me. You need to be thinking more along the lines of, I don't know... Oh, I've got it. Think along the lines of artist on a date."

"Artist on a date?" She blurts out a loud laugh. "What does that entail? A paint smattered smock, and my hair all tied up in bright rags?"

"No, it means kind of bohemian but a bit sexy. Like, you're cool, and a little bit different and kooky, but still hot for it? But not hot for it on that actual night. Coz he's gotta work for that, yeah?"

"Bitch, I've been thirsting after this guy for so long that I don't know how hard he's going to have to work for it. I'm going to have to do all the work. I'm going to have to work to lock lady libido right down so I don't rip his pants off the first chance I get."

"You know the rule."

She laughs. "I know the rule. No giving it away on the first date."

The door opens, and Asher walks in, tapping a metaphorical watch on his wrist.

"I've got to go, honey," I say.

"I've missed you so much. I really hope we can speak soon. And you better check those pictures in a couple of nights and tell me which outfit looks most suitable. What was it you said again? Oh, yeah, artist on a date." She giggles and as is still giggling as she signs off with, "Love you, babe."

"Love you right back."

I end the call and pass the phone back to Asher.

He takes it from me without a word.

"Thanks so much for that. I really do appreciate it more than you can know. I miss her."

"You're welcome," he says, but there's something dark to his tone. As if I did something wrong.

"Asher?" I ask, not sure what the hell I've done this time to upset him.

"Get some rest, Honor. Tomorrow will be a busy day."

He gives me his patented, nasty-boy smirk and gathers up the laptop, exiting without saying another word.

Dick.

But nothing can stop my good mood now.

I spoke to my friend, and it was amazing, and nothing can diminish that shine.

Chapter Eleven
Asher

I STALK BACK DOWN THE corridor toward the main living area, my mood as sour as the gummy bear I'm sucking. The weirdest urge to grab Honor overcame me just now. It's as if by chatting to her friend, she's shown me an innocent, almost childlike side of herself, and I needed to erase that.

I should never have listened in to the phone call and watched her on the screens.

I'm such a fucking idiot. I didn't know that I could fully trust her, so I listened in case anything was said that I needed to stop.

She was herself on that call, though. And she seemed different. Lighter. Happier. Even more beautiful when her face lights up in real joy. I shouldn't have watched it. Not when it means I have come to see Honor more as a fully-fledged, rounded human being than a fuck toy.

I never let myself see women that way. People might think that's sexist or misogynistic, but it's the truth. I see women as either people who work for me, or the mother who betrayed me and let me down when she sent me to that Godawful church of Pastor Wren's, or as my pathetic sister who didn't believe me when I told her what Pastor Wren was doing to me.

Worse, she denied I ever told her when I finally tried to tell the authorities. She painted me as a liar.

Yeah, these are the women who represent womanhood to me. Then there were all the simpering bitches who were just receptacles for my anger and aggression through my teen years, when my rage was at its peak. The worse I treated them, the more they wanted me. It made me pretty damn convinced that women are fucked up and broken.

Lying sisters. Useless mothers who don't do their job. Bitches who want your cock or your money.

Those are the people that women are to me.

There's not a woman on this Earth who has ever shown me that she's anything beyond either greedy, sex hungry, money hungry, or untrustworthy.

One might say it's ironic that Pastor Wren is the person who hurt me the most, and yet I don't hate men, I hate women. It's not ironic, though, because I found three really good friends in Rafferty, Brody, and Wilder. I also had great friends through high school. In fact, it was my friends who kept me sane enough that I didn't actually end it all by jumping off the school roof.

But when the person you're supposed to be able to trust the most in the world, your own fucking mother, lets you down unequivocally, it's hard to trust women. Especially when that followed on the heels of further letdowns by your sister, teachers, and every girl you get any vague feelings for in the next few years.

BRUTAL LIMITS 119

No, Pastor Wren is a piece of crap who must die. But so far, in my experience of the world, he's an outlier.

Whereas the shitty women I've met have been the rule, not the exception.

Now, though, there's Honor. Somehow, along the way, she's becoming a lot more than just a simple toy for me to play with.

Is almost as if she is becoming a part of our group.

We can't let that happen.

Panic grips me at the thought. If she becomes a part of the group, she will come between us. Absolutely guaranteed.

I'm torn. Earlier today, the idea of her leaving had me in pieces. Not because I love her, or any of the other reasons that Rafferty clearly thinks I want her to stay for. No, I want her to stay so I can play with her a little longer. She's the most delicious creature we've played this game with.

Now, though, if I think of her staying, it gives me fear. I might not see her as the love of my life, but I'm starting to think Wilder might. Even Rafferty, possibly. Which is a head fuck, because I thought that guy was a robot.

Brody doesn't. Brody knew from the start that she couldn't be trusted.

To me, she was never anything more than a bit of fun. Someone to be played with, and toyed with, and degraded if I so wished. But now I've gone and listened to that conversation, and she's far too terrifyingly like a whole person to me.

She seemed so young. So much younger than she is when we've played our games. I know that she's not much older than her early twenties. It's been easy to fool myself that she's as jaded as we are because she's playing the same game, and she wants the money at the end of it.

However, that conversation proves she is far from jaded. She's a young woman who's in over her head.

When her friend mentioned her stepfather, Honor's reaction was genuine. I was watching her face on the monitor, and I could see the real fear in her eyes.

What has that fucker done to her? There's something burning in my gut, and I don't know what it is. A new emotion I can't place.

The way she talked and laughed so lightheartedly with her friend has touched me, I can't lie. I don't want to feel this way. I don't want to let anyone in but these three men I trust.

I think the world is far too dark a place for anything approaching romantic love to be real. I tell myself it's nothing like that that I'm feeling. It's simply a non-romantic, normal attachment to a human being who I'm letting myself get to know.

But I don't feel attachments, do I? I mean, even to these guys, there's not a real attachment there or I wouldn't have the plans I do for when this is all finished and we've taken our revenge.

I could walk away from this right now and start all over again with a minimal amount of pain to myself.

At the last minute, I change course, and instead of heading back into the living area, I go back to the room where the monitors are.

I need to watch her again for a moment. That's a part of me that needs to see if what I'm feeling is what I think it is. Something horrifyingly close to affection.

I place the laptop down and watch the screen in front of me. I expected to see Honor alone, but Felicity is in the room. She must have arrived just after I left.

She's clearing the empty crockery onto a tray. That's odd. Something like that isn't Felicity's job. I frown and flick my gaze between Felicity and Honor. The body language of both women is all wrong. While they've never exactly been friends, I'd always gotten the impression they muscled along together all right. Right now, however, Felicity is square shouldered and slamming plates down onto the tray, and Honor has reared away, worry written all over her pretty features.

Felicity says something, and I listen carefully.

"I can't believe you're still here, you conniving little bitch." Felicity purses her thin lips and gives Honor a nakedly aggressive stare.

What the hell? The woman is overstepping her role somewhat, isn't she?

"It's nothing to do with you," Honor says.

I smile to myself, proud of our girl for standing up for herself.

"It's got everything to do with me. I've worked here for a long time, and let me tell you, I've never seen such a sneaky little bitch as you. I can't wait until you're gone. They must be going soft in the head to let you stay."

"They'd be angry to hear you talk about them in such a manner," Honor says.

She's not fucking wrong.

Felicity pulls her hand back and slaps Honor so hard across her face that Honor stumbles. She loses her footing and falls, hitting the side of her face on a chair. The crack is audible through the monitor speakers, and I jerk back in shock. Honor goes slack, and I find my breath trapped in my chest. It's not until Honor moves again that I release the air from my lungs.

I gape at the screen, not believing what I'm seeing. Felicity has lost her mind.

"Oh, my God," Honor cries.

She pulls herself upright but remains on the floor. Her cheek is covered in blood and already darkening with a bruise.

Pure blinding rage, the likes of which I haven't felt for a long time, fills me.

Felicity stands over her. "You better tell those men you tripped and fell, or I'll fucking make sure you have a much worse accident. You need to leave. You're not wanted here." Felicity grabs Honor's ponytail and yanks it so hard, Honor screams.

"Say a word, and you're dead."

I'm moving before I can stop myself.

Chapter Twelve
Honor

FELICITY GIVES MY PONYTAIL another yank, pain spearing through my scalp. I yelp and clutch both hands to my head, as though trying to keep my hair in place. Mercifully, she releases me, but I'm sure she's taken a chunk of my hair with her.

My cheekbone throbs, and I touch my fingers to my face. When I pull them back again, blood coats the tips.

I don't think I've ever had my mood swing so rapidly from one pole to another. One moment, I was on a high after talking to Ruth, and the next, Felicity had barged in here. I could tell right away that something was very wrong.

I have to admit, I haven't given Felicity much thought since the guys found out about my lie. They're the ones who've crowded out my thoughts every second of every day. Felicity was the one who'd had me sign the contract, though, so perhaps the mistake and my lie had gotten her into trouble. It hadn't been something I had considered. She wasn't to blame, after all, but perhaps the guys hadn't seen things that way. I don't know what they've said to her in private, but whatever it was, she's clearly decided I'm the one at fault.

I guess she's not wrong about that.

Whatever I might have done, I never deserved for her to come in and attack me. Was it my comment about the men not wanting to hear her talking about them in such a way that pushed her over the edge, or had this always been in the cards?

My limbs tremble as I pull myself to my feet. My ears buzz, but I can't tell if it's from the slap, or hitting my head, or if it's just the result of all the adrenaline rushing through my veins. I clench my fists, holding myself back from launching at her and giving her back some of what she's just dealt me. The only thing that's stopping me is the thought of how the men will react if they learn I've attacked one of their top employees, even if it is in self-defense.

I can't give them another reason to throw me off the island early.

It occurs to me that might be what Felicity's plan has been all along. Maybe she wants me to retaliate so she has a reason to get the men to throw me out.

I suck in a steadying breath and glare at her, waiting for her next move. Her eyes are steely flints, and I see no remorse in them. She fixes on my bleeding cheek, and a slow smile curves one side of her lips.

Will she come at me again?

She takes a step toward me, but, to my left, the door flies open with a bang as though someone has kicked it from the other side, and Asher flies into the room.

I have a flash where I picture him joining Felicity in her violence toward me, knocking me back to the ground and pinning me down. Maybe he's finally decided to make me pay. But instead of heading toward me, it's Felicity he goes to.

One shove against her narrow chest sends her flying to the ground, and then he's on top of her, his hands wrapped around her throat.

"You don't fucking touch Honor," he snarls. "She's ours."

He gives her neck a shake, and her head whips back and forth like a ragdoll.

No matter what she's done to me, I don't want to see her hurt.

"Asher!" I scream. "Stop it! Get off her!"

It occurs to me that Asher must have seen Felicity hitting me. If he'd watched that, did that mean he'd also watched or listened in on my conversation with Ruth? I'm relieved I didn't say anything to her about any of the men.

I can't worry about that now. I'm more worried that Asher is about to kill Felicity.

Feeling like I have no choice, I jump on his back, using my entire body weight to pull him off. He's so much stronger than I am, however, and he barely even seems to notice I'm there. I yank and tug at his shoulders, but his hands remained around Felicity's throat, though he seems to be shaking her more than strangling her. Her eyes bulge, and her face is red, but she still seems to be breathing. I'm pretty sure if Asher wanted her dead, she'd be dead already. Is he just taking his time about it? Making sure she understands exactly what she's done wrong before he finally tightens his fingers that last little bit?

I realize I'm not strong enough to stop him. I need help.

I climb off Asher and run for the door, bursting out into the corridor.

"Help!" I scream. "Someone help!"

I run, as fast as I can, my feet bare against the plush carpet. I have no idea where I'll find the others—they might not even be in the building, for all I know. It occurs to me that the men all most likely have private bedrooms or living quarters of their own, but I've never been shown them, and I don't know where they are. All I can do is make my best guess as to the guys' locations, and that is going to be the office or else the dining room. Since the office is closest, I head there, but I'm screaming for help the whole way, praying someone will hear me. I don't even care if it's not one of the guys. I'd take the pool cleaner or even one of the maids at this point.

I burst into the office and almost sob with relief when I find Wilder in there.

"He's going to kill her," I cry. "Please, you have to come."

Wilder frowns at me and rises to his feet, dwarfing me with his form. "What the fuck are you talking about?" His gaze lands on my face and the cut that's currently trickling blood down to my jaw. "And what happened to your face?"

There's no time to stand around discussing this. I lunge forward and grab his arm, trying to pull him with me, but it's like trying to move a mountain.

"Asher is killing Felicity. Please, Wilder, you have to come."

His green eyes widen slightly as it dawns on him that I'm not screwing around. I sag with relief as he sets off toward the door.

"Where?" he demands.

"My room."

Wilder takes off at a run, and I struggle to keep up. His long legs mean I have to take two strides for every one of his. He's also strong and healthy, while I'm bleeding, have been slapped, and possibly have a concussion. I can't worry about any of that right now, though. I'm so distressed at the possibility that Asher might kill someone on my behalf that everything else fades into the background.

He won't kill her, will he? I try to convince myself. *He's a little crazy, but not murderously so.*

I'm not sure I'll ever get over the guilt if we're too late. I know I can't control these men or blame myself for their actions, but the death of my mother already sits heavy in my heart—I'm constantly questioning if I could have done more to prevent it—and I don't think I've got the strength to take on the murder of another woman.

Wilder reaches the room several seconds before I do. He vanishes through the door. My breath catches, and I want to cry again. I don't want to go in there, but at the same time, I can't stand out here and not know what's happening. I strain my ears, hoping the shouts from inside will give me some clue as to what's happening, but they're too muffled to pick up on the words.

I force myself to enter.

Wilder has already hauled Asher off Felicity, and now it's Asher's turn to be shaken like a rag doll.

"Get the fuck off me," Asher spits at Wilder.

To my relief, Felicity has rolled to her stomach and is commando crawling away from the men. She's definitely still alive.

The men are now fighting each other, so I go to her, crouching beside her, and reach out to touch her shoulder. "Felicity, are you all right?"

She turns to me with raw hatred in her bloodshot eyes and yanks herself away. "Don't you fucking touch me!"

I gasp at the vehemence in her tone. It's not as though I'm the one who's hurt her. I'm bleeding because of her, not the other way around.

"I was just making sure you were all right," I mutter.

She must see me as the person who's come between her and her four bosses. Did she think she was something special to them? Even though she must have watched numerous girls coming and going, she was always their one constant. I'd always considered her being so much older that it never occurred to me that she might have thought of any of them in such a way, but I guess both Wilder and Rafferty are probably closer to her in age than they are to me. I mean, they're both gorgeous, so why wouldn't she have developed feelings for them over time? She must have consoled herself with the fact that the girls they brought here always left after only a few days, yet I was still here, and currently wasn't going anywhere. Or maybe I was overthinking it and it was simply that she didn't like that I'd lied to her and, in her mind, got away with it.

That might be the truth, but this felt personal. It wasn't just about a lie or a contract.

She was jealous.

"Breathe, Asher," Wilder says, still not releasing his grip. "Fucking breathe."

Asher's gaze flicks over Wilder's shoulder and locks on to me. "That bitch made Honor bleed. She fucking made her *bleed*. She needs to pay."

"You've already made her pay," Wilder says. "Felicity knows she did wrong, don't you, Felicity?"

Felicity wheezes and coughs. "You're fucking crazy."

Asher lunges for her again, but Wilder's superior strength holds him back. I'm so relieved I found him when I did.

"Apologize to Honor," Wilder growls at Felicity. "Then Asher will chill the fuck out. Won't you, Asher?"

Asher only scowls, but he doesn't argue with Wilder. I guess an apology will be enough for him as well.

Felicity's jaw locks, and she clearly doesn't want to.

"She doesn't have to apologize," I say, desperately wanting to smooth things over. "I probably deserved it."

"Don't get involved, Honor," Wilder snaps.

I press my lips shut. I think I'm about as involved as it's possible to be, but I don't want to start any more fights. I already feel as though I'm screwing things up. I need this money, and it's clear the men still want to play their games with me, but it was never my intention to come into this and rock their boat.

I never wanted anyone to get hurt.

Wilder still hasn't let go of Asher. "If you're not going to apologize to Honor," he directs his words at Felicity, "I suggest you pack your bags and get the plane to take you to the mainland."

"She doesn't have—" I start, but one look from him shuts me up again.

Felicity manages to get to her feet. "Don't worry, I'm going. If you think I'm staying a moment longer with you bunch of psychopaths, you can think again. I'll happily be out of your hair. But you're making a mistake. This little bitch is going to be your downfall, the whole lot of you."

I still feel bad for her, no matter what she says. I don't know exactly how long she's worked for them all, but it must be some time. Plus, this isn't just her place of work, it's also her home. I know what it's like to feel like you no longer have a place to call your own—to be so unsettled, wandering, not belonging anywhere. But then I remember the shoes Felicity was wearing the first day I arrived here, and how they were worth more than the whole sum total of my belongings. Maybe she wouldn't have a home here, but since she was clearly well paid and didn't have many expenses on the island, I assumed she'd have a tidy nest egg all saved up.

With her hand at her throat, and shooting me a final look of hatred, she stalks from the room, slamming the door shut behind her.

Chapter Thirteen
Wilder

I UNDERSTAND WHY THE blood on Honor's face set Asher off so badly.

I felt it myself—the surge of protectiveness rising inside me, the urge to destroy anyone and anything who might do that to her. I like to think I'd have managed to be more restrained than Asher, but if I'd witnessed Honor getting hurt like that, I definitely couldn't have promised anything.

Now Felicity is out of the room, I risk letting Asher go. He yanks himself away from me and brushes himself down. I study his face, ensuring that ice-cold wall he puts up when he's like this has thoroughly melted. It's impossible to get through to him when he's got that shielding his heart—it's like trying to talk to someone I don't even recognize. I'm relieved to see he's back again.

"We need to tell Rafferty what's happened," I say. "Brody, too."

"In a minute," Asher replies. "First we need to look after her."

We both turn toward Honor. The cut on her face has started to clot, the blood darkening and thickening. More blood is smeared across her skin and has run in tracks down to her jaw. A port-wine bruise is already forming on her cheekbone, and I have no doubt that it'll be black and blue by tomorrow.

"Are you okay?" I ask her.

To my surprise, she nods, but then bursts into tears.

"I'm sorry," she sobs. "I'm sorry. I'm sorry."

I act before I even think, finding myself scooping her into my arms and carefully holding her poor injured face against my chest, not caring if I get blood on my shirt.

"Shush," I try to soothe her, stroking her hair. "You don't have anything to be sorry for."

"Yes, I do. I ruined everything. I lied, and now Felicity has to leave, and it's all my fault."

I remain silent but continue to run my palm over her hair. It's not like she's wrong, but it's not all on her, either.

Eventually, it's Asher who speaks.

"We're the ones who decided to let you stay. And how I act isn't on you, baby girl. Don't ever think that."

She sniffs and nods against me. I lean away from her slightly to get a better look at her face, but she tries to burrow back into me, as though ashamed. I catch her chin in my fingers and force her eyes to mine.

The sight of the blood against that perfect white skin fills me with fury. I hope Felicity has the good sense to get off the island quickly before the others find out as well.

Honor gazes up at me, her blue eyes still teary. Her lips are parted slightly, and she takes a shaky breath.

I don't know why I do it, but I lower my mouth to hers and kiss her. For a moment, the kiss is almost chaste, even serene, just a placing of lips against lips. But then her tongue tentatively touches mine, and the action sets off an avalanche of arousal. I remember how it felt to have her sweet pussy surrounding my cock, and I deepen the kiss, sliding my tongue over hers and crushing her small, curvy body against mine.

I remember she's injured and force myself away.

"Stop, wait. You're hurt."

"I'm okay," she insists.

"No, you're not." I take her by the hand and lead her into the bathroom. My cock is thick and heavy against my thigh, already engorged with blood. My piercing moves around the harder I get, grazing the sensitive tissue and stimulating the pleasurable nerves. It's incredible how just being around her, even when she's fully dressed and there's nothing going on, affects me. Her fingers are tiny and delicate in my huge palm, and I get a waft of her freshly washed hair and the signature scent we've given her.

Maybe we should be pleased that Felicity hurt her, punished her. Wasn't that what we wanted—for her to pay for lying to us? But I can't take any satisfaction in this, and I don't think any of the others will either. Seeing her hurt is doing things to me I'd never even considered before. Her pain is my pain, which is a hell of a thing to realize. Maybe we aren't as in control of this as we like to think anymore.

I sit her on the edge of the tub and go to the medicine cabinet to see what I can find. We have first aid kits elsewhere in the building, and I'll go and get one if I can't find what I need here. Asher has followed us in and now stands propped in the doorway, his arms folded across his chest as he watches. I'm pleased he's come with us. At least I can keep an eye on him and know that he's not chasing after Felicity to end what he started.

No, he wouldn't kill her. If he'd wanted her dead, then she'd be dead already.

I find some rubbing alcohol, cotton balls, and Steri-Strips. They should do the job.

Working carefully, I clean up Honor's cheek. She hisses air over her teeth and winces as the alcohol makes contact with the wound but doesn't complain.

"You are being so brave," I tell her. "And you did the right thing, coming to me when Ash was..." I trail off, not wanting to end my sentence.

Asher steps forward. "I'm sorry if I frightened you, Honor. That was never my intention."

She closes her eyes briefly. "It wasn't only me you frightened. It was Felicity, too."

Asher shakes his head. "She deserved it."

"Not like that."

Honor is probably right, but I don't want to start another argument between us all.

"Hold still," I tell her as I apply the Steri-Strips.

She does as I say, and I finish up. The cut isn't as bad as it looked at first glance, especially after the blood has been cleaned away, but she's still going to have one hell of a bruise in the morning.

"All done."

She offers me a hint of a smile. "Thanks, Wilder."

"You're welcome, Snow." I look to Asher. "And how are you?"

His jaw tightens. "Fine."

He's clearly not fine. Tension is radiating from him, and he needs a release. Honor is hurt, and it's dark, so it's not as though I'm going to send her across the island with Asher in the state he's in, chasing after her. For the first time, I wish we had another girl here who he could get his release with instead, but I don't know how either Asher or Honor would react to that. From the way he's looking at her, I've got the feeling that no other girl would do, and I wonder what Honor's reaction would be to any of us fucking someone else. Would she be jealous? We've done nothing to warm her to us, so she'd most likely be relieved if we took on a new girl. Not that we want to right now. In a few days, however, we won't have any choice. She'll be leaving, so either we find someone new at some point in the future or we stay celibate forever.

Neither option sounds like a good one.

Honor looks to Asher. "I'm sorry I put you in that situation. If I'd kept my mouth shut with Felicity, or had never lied in the first place, you wouldn't have felt the need to go for her."

This is all feeling a bit too much like victim blaming for my liking.

"Asher knows what he did is on him," I say. "Don't you, Ash?"

He nods. "Yeah. I just reacted. Sorry, Honor."

She looks like she can barely believe Asher is actually apologizing for something. To be honest, I'm pretty shocked myself. I try to think of the last time I've ever heard him say sorry, and I can't think of even one. I'm not sure any of us have ever really apologized for anything we've done. We're not that kind of people—not that I'm saying that's a good thing.

She gets to her feet and goes to him. "I don't like seeing you like that. You frighten me. You're still frightening me now."

He ducks his head as though in shame. "I don't mean to." Christ, who is this man, and where is the sullen, hardened Ash I know?

She lifts her hand and places her palm to his cheek. "I don't understand you."

"I don't think I understand me either."

She might not understand him, but right now, she's giving him what he needs. With her touch, I watch the muscles in his neck and shoulders loosen, the tension releasing from his jaw. She seems to sense it, too, as she runs her hand from his face around to his nape, lacing her fingers in his hair. With her other hand, she takes off his black framed glasses and sets them to one side on the dresser. Then she stands on tiptoes and kisses him, much in the same way I'd kissed her only minutes earlier, calm and serene. Asher's eyes slip shut, and his body relaxes further.

It occurs to me that it might be considered strange how Honor is comforting Asher, when she's the one who's hurt, but then I realize they're both hurting, just in different ways.

Their kiss deepens, growing more passionate. As I watch, my cock hardens again. I know this isn't about me, however, so I stay where I am. I'm more than happy to watch.

Asher's hands fist into her hair and then run a languid trail down her spine to rest on her ass. He grabs her bottom and drags her harder against him. She lets out a moan, and from the way she's moving, I can tell she's grinding against his cock.

I press my forearm to my own erection and push my hips forward. A rush of pleasure goes through me, blood heating my face. Watching these two grinding on each other is already doing things to me, and, by the look of things, it's only going to get hotter.

Asher yanks down her bottoms and G-string, exposing the perfect curves of her backside. She kicks the items off her feet. Still kissing with frantic nips and bites, he lifts her and places her on the cabinet where she put his glasses only moments earlier. He sweeps them away with his hand, seemingly not caring if they break. He pushes her thighs apart and adjusts himself between them. Though his back blocks the view, I can tell he's pulled out his dick. From their movements and the expression of sheer bliss that crosses Honor's face, it's obvious when he pushes inside her.

I pull out my cock and flick the piercing, relishing the little electric shocks of intensity it gives me. I move my hand up and down my length, enjoying the little show Honor and Asher are putting on. I know it's not for my benefit, but they're both fully aware I'm here. Not that they seem to care. I definitely wish I could get in on the action. I move my hand faster and faster, taking myself back to earlier that day when it was me inside her. She'd done so well taking my full girth, and I wonder how far we'll be able to take her. Will she one day be able to take both me and Rafferty, or me and one of the others, at the same time in that sweet pussy? I hope so.

He pushes up her top and yanks down her bra. Roughly, he cups one of her breasts. Her tits bounce every time he thrusts into her. Her calves are hooked around his hips, and his ass muscles are bunched tight.

"Asher, wait," she says suddenly. "We haven't used a condom."

"Fuck," he growls. "Just give me a little more time."

His hips move as he continues to fuck her bare.

"Oh, God," she groans.

I understand why he wants that so badly. Hadn't I done the same thing? Feeling her pussy so wet and hot surrounding your dick has got to be one of the most incredible sensations out there.

We're always safe with the girls we bring here. We always wear condoms one hundred percent of the time. It's never even needed to be discussed. Yet here we are with her, each of us wanting to get inside her, to feel her fully.

It's a good thing Rafferty put her on that birth control. If we're going to keep her, she's going to need it.

I shake the thought from my head, wondering where it's come from. We're not keeping her. She's not some injured bird we've brought home to nurse back to health.

"Asher," she says, breathing hard but with a warning in her tone.

"Fuck, you feel so good, baby girl." He sucks in air. "You're like coming home."

Does he mean that?

A new pang of worry goes through me. What if this is too much? Though I've wanted Asher to feel something akin to human for a long time now, I also worry about what will happen if he gets attached to someone and then they leave. How will he hold himself together? I've already seen tonight how messed up he is. Though I'm strong, there had been a definite moment where I'd been worried I wouldn't be able to get him off Felicity.

"I won't come, I swear. I just want to you feel you."

"Asher," she says again, her voice stern. "Condom. Now."

I wonder if he's going to listen to her, and hope I'm not going to have to pull him off a second woman tonight, though if I do, I'll happily take his place.

But he listens. "Fuck."

He pulls out and takes a condom from his back pocket—we know to always be prepared—rips open the package, and rolls it down his erection. Then he's back inside her again.

She peers at me from over his shoulder as he ducks his head to lick and suck and bite her nipples. She laces her fingers in his hair and moans, but the whole time she's looking at me. Fuck, it's hot the way she's doing that. I don't experience any jealousy at her being with Asher while I only get to watch. Maybe I should, but that's not how things work between us.

The sounds of their fucking grow louder.

"Oh, God." She gives a breathy moan. "Oh, yes...fuck, yes."

Honor is braced with both palms on the dresser, her head tilted up, tits skyward, as Asher rams into her. Then they're coming together, and I do, too, hot semen spurting from the end of my cock, raining down onto the floor.

I wish Honor's pretty mouth had been there to catch it.

Chapter Fourteen
Honor

I PULL MY TOP AND BRA back into place and scoop up my panties and bottoms with my foot. I catch Wilder's eye from the other side of the bathroom, and he throws me a wink. My cheeks heat.

Asher puts himself back together, too. I want him to look at me, to acknowledge that what just happened between us was as close to intimacy as we've ever had. But in true Asher style, he slips his glasses back on and turns from me as though I'm not even there.

Wilder has also straightened himself up. "We need to tell Rafferty and Brody what just happened."

I widen my eyes. "Do they have to know about *that*?" As soon as the words are out of my mouth, I realize he doesn't mean the sex.

Wilder chuckles. "I meant what happened with Felicity."

I can't look at him. "Yeah, of course. Should I come with you?"

"I think you should. They need to see what she did. It doesn't feel real if you haven't seen it in the flesh, as it were."

I know he's right, but I'm still nervous. I don't want Rafferty or Brody to hold me to blame for them losing Felicity. I also don't want anything to ruin the strange kind of truce I seem to have reached with Wilder and Asher, either. I know it's tenuous and things could flip back to how they were at any moment, but, in these last few minutes, we've felt like a team.

Together, we leave my room and follow Asher back down the corridor.

"I know how to find them," he says.

He leads us to a room that's wall to wall with monitors. I gaze around, recognizing different areas of the resort—the pool, the dining room, the kitchens. This must be the security room.

Asher quickly crosses to the control board and flicks some of the switches, but not before I catch sight of my bedroom on one of the screens.

"You've been watching me?" I say.

He shrugs. "It was in the contract, remember? No privacy."

The contract that apparently doesn't count anymore, I think but don't say.

When I don't respond, he turns back to the screens. "There they are."

I follow his line of sight to what appears to be a cinema room, though the lights are up, so I assume they're not watching anything yet. There are only about eight chairs—each one big enough to lie almost horizontal—with large cup and snack holders attached to each arm. Occupying two of them are Rafferty and Brody.

I find myself fascinated. Though they must know they're on camera—after all, Rafferty was probably the one who ordered them—they both seem completely relaxed. They have a large tub of popcorn each and are casually chucking pieces at each other and laughing. It's addictive to see them like this, unarmed and with their walls completely down. Was this how Asher felt when he was watching me?

"We know where to find them," Wilder says, turning and leaving the room.

I draw a breath and follow, Asher close behind.

We head down, right into the bowels of the building. The door to the cinema room is padded for soundproofing, and the lights have been lowered now. As we push in, the loud music of the opening credits hits my ears. They must have started their movie.

"Sorry to interrupt," Wilder says, hitting a light switch to illuminate the room again, "but this is important."

Rafferty sits up. "What the fuck, Wilder?"

He notices I'm here, too, and raises both eyebrows. In the other seat, Brody hits some kind of remote, and the movie pauses.

Brody must have spotted my injury. "What the fuck happened to you?"

"Felicity," Asher says, not giving me the chance to answer for myself. "She attacked Honor."

Brody's expression hardens. "Why?"

"She didn't like that Honor was allowed to stay even after we'd discovered she'd lied."

Rafferty stands. "Then she should have come to us with that issue, not Honor. Where is she now?"

"Off the island, I hope," Asher says. "We told her to leave."

Wilder shoots him a look. "That's not all. Do you want to tell them, or shall I?"

Rafferty's lips thin. "Tell us what?"

A muscle twitches beside Asher's eye. "I might have lost my shit with her. I...did what I do."

"You strangled her?" Rafferty confirms.

"Only a little."

Rafferty looks to me and Wilder. "Only a little bit?" he checks.

I bite my lower lip, feeling traitorous, but aware that Rafferty needs to know everything. "I couldn't get Asher off her. I had to run to get Wilder."

"Good thing she did, too," Wilder says.

"Smart girl." Brody nods approvingly.

I'm not so sure about that, but I appreciate the praise.

"I'm sorry she hurt you," Rafferty tells me. "That should never have happened. Are you okay now?"

I nod. "Wilder patched me up, and Asher...made me feel better."

Rafferty arches an eyebrow. "Asher made you feel better?"

Wilder smirks. "Looks like our boy has his moments."

My stomach knots, worried they'll want more details, but they move on.

Rafferty directs his next words at Brody. "Can you make sure Felicity has left the island?"

"Will do."

He leaves the cinema room.

Rafferty sits back again, his fingers steepled at his chin. "We need to talk about you losing it, Asher. Do we have to worry about you?"

"No," he replies quickly, perhaps too quickly. "I'm fine."

Rafferty doesn't seem to believe him. "You need to work out that tension. We should do a new hunt tomorrow."

He doesn't know that Asher's just fucked me for the second time that day. I'm starting to understand that this isn't all about the sex, though. Sex is only a part of it. I remember how I was unsettled and restless in the room before I'd called Ruth, and I wonder if that's how Asher—and maybe the others, too—feel when they haven't done a hunt for some time. A chase across the island uses muscles and energy that normal day-to-day living simply doesn't, and then there's the thrill and adrenaline that come with it.

They don't need my consent to do another hunt, but I give it anyway. "I'll be up for it in the morning."

Rafferty nods. "Good to know. The hunt will be on tomorrow, then." He settles back in his seat. "Now, who's up for watching this?"

He's taken this way better than I'd given him credit for, but I don't dare to relax just yet. Maybe my punishment will come tomorrow when the next game starts.

I turn to head for the door to go back to my room.

Rafferty's voice rings out. "Where are you going?"

I freeze. "Umm, back to my room?"

"You don't want to join us for the movie? You might not like it, mind you. It's a horror."

I find my cheeks twitching. "I love horror. It's my favorite movie genre."

He raises his eyebrows in surprise and then pats the reclined seat beside him. "Better get comfortable, then."

Brody re-enters the room and throws himself back into his seat. "She's gone."

"Good." Rafferty sniffs. "She'd better not be thinking about causing us any trouble."

"She can't," Asher says. "She's been complicit in everything we've done here. You had her sign and NDA too, and if she does talk, we can sue."

Rafferty nods, and his shoulders relax a notch.

I hope they're right.

Brody picks up his popcorn and throws a kernel at me. It hits me on the head and bounces off.

"Hey," I protest, though I'm smiling. "No fair. I don't have anything to retaliate with."

Rafferty pushes his tub of popcorn into my hands. "Knock yourself out."

Someone lowers the lights again, and the movie restarts. I pop a piece of corn into my mouth, enjoying the sweet and salty taste, and snuggle down into my seat. Though my face still throbs, and the knot of worry in my stomach still hasn't completely gone, I find myself relaxing.

I know to make the most of this.

Tomorrow, a new hunt will start, and then everything will change once again.

Chapter Fifteen
Honor

I SLEEP WELL DESPITE the drama of yesterday. The next morning, I awaken feeling lighter than I have in a long time. Although what happened was upsetting, I can't lie, I'm relieved that Felicity has gone. My cheek hurts, and I touch it gently, wincing as it throbs in protest at even the lightest of touches. Rafferty found me some painkillers, so I take a couple, washing them down with the water left on my nightstand.

I still can't quite believe how badly Felicity lost it. It's like she became crazed. She always seemed so calm and in control. It just goes to show that you never really know another person.

Then there's Asher. Now, his reaction wasn't exactly a surprise. A shock, perhaps. No one wants to witness a person almost getting throttled to death. However, I cannot truthfully say it took me by surprise.

I've been wary of Asher ever since he showed me his true self, and I think perhaps I always will be to a degree. Even if, somehow, I stayed here longer than the next few days, and became friends with some of the guys, I think I would always have a healthy respect for Asher's temper.

Never mind Brody. I still don't think that man has forgiven me at all. He seemed to be the least perturbed out of all four of them about the cut high on my cheek.

For some reason, he's still angry at me, and he can't let it go the way the others have.

I wish I knew their secrets. I wish I could see inside their minds and find out what makes them tick. They're all such enigmas in different ways.

There's a knock on my door, and for a brief second, I tense, my body reacting as if Felicity is still going to be the one to sweep into the room giving me commands. It's not, though, of course. A young man walks in and places a tray groaning with food, coffee, and orange juice down on the table.

I give him my thanks and settle down to eat a healthy breakfast. It's always a tricky balance when I know there's going to be a hunt, between filling myself up enough to have energy, and not overfilling myself so I can't run without getting a cramp.

Today, I choose to have some yogurt with berries. I also nibble on a couple of slices of bacon for the protein. I wash it all down with the orange juice, and then, when I'm finished, dab my mouth with the thick linen napkin and sip at the delicious coffee.

I remember to take my pill as well, the same way I did yesterday. It's been forty-eight hours now, so I guess that means it'll have started to work. Though I didn't appreciate the way Rafferty went about it, I do appreciate the extra protection. Though the guys have generally been good about using condoms, they can always split, and it hasn't escaped my notice that they've been wanting to be inside me bare more and more.

I do understand why—nothing beats that intimacy of skin on skin—but I'm too young for babies, and bringing a child into this situation would be all kinds of fucked up.

I take another sip of my coffee and sigh with pleasure.

Imagine living like this all the time. The luxury of this place is stupendous. The food is delicious. Even the orange juice is fresh with chunky bits of real orange in it. Everything about the place runs like clockwork and is made to ensure that anyone here has a wonderful experience.

I've never been one to be bothered by *things*. Material goods aren't something I yearn for, but this is the other side of what money can buy you. A life that runs like clockwork with only the best things to eat and drink.

Then there's the travel.

After being on a Greyhound for hours on end, I could honestly say that the idea of traveling first class is not something I would turn my nose up at. If I were rich, I wouldn't waste my money on handbags and stupid shoes, or all the other things people spend their money on—the sort of stuff Felicity obviously spends her money on. No, I'd spend my money on experiences. My luxuries would be paying for upper class travel, and gorgeous hotel rooms with fluffy robes, and starched bed linens.

When you have slept in the bus station, you do truly appreciate luxury once you have it.

After eating, I dress myself in the way I always do when it's a hunt. The Lara Croft outfit, as I think of it. I pull my hair up tight and let the ponytail swing high. I know the reason for the ponytail—it's so they've got something to hold on to.

I apply a spritz of the signature scent, because the one thing I have to give Felicity her due for is that the woman has a good nose. This scent is utterly delicious, and I think I've become addicted to it. I breath it in and sigh happily. I'm tempted to ask the men if I can take a bottle with me when I leave.

Sadness washes over me at that thought, gripping my stomach in a vice. I push it away, needing to focus. I apply a tiny amount of makeup to distract myself. There's not much point really in making an effort because in about thirty minutes, I will be a sweaty, hot mess. Still, my vanity has me brushing some bronzer over my cheeks, my decolletage, and my nose, before I add a swipe of mascara and some colored lip balm.

I check my reflection in the mirror and notice I'm gaining muscle tone in my arms. I've not been working out in any sort of traditional sense, but I've been running, climbing up rocks, and scrambling about this island, and I expect I've lost a little bit of body weight and gained some muscle. Suits me. If only I could get something of a tan. I've always had such pale skin.

I give myself one last glance and exit the room.

By the time I enter the main living area, all the men have gathered.

Four sets of eyes appraise me, and I find myself standing taller, sucking in my stomach and pushing out my breasts. I hate how I'm still seeking their approval and attention, even after everything, but I can't help it. I'm hungry for it. I've been alone for so long that feeling as though I'm part of this group, no matter how fucked up, fills me with longing.

A smile quirks Asher's lip. "Looking good, baby girl."

I flash him a small smile of thanks.

Brody is staring at me, his gaze hard. I find myself shrinking under it.

Rafferty clears his throat. "We need to do things properly today."

"Properly?"

I'm unsure what that means.

"We're doing a hunt, but there'll be no prize at the end, no chance of you actually winning."

My stomach drops. "Oh."

"We will catch you, princess," he says.

"Then...then what's the point in me running?"

If all they want to do is fuck me, we can do that right here, right now. Why bother with the whole charade?

Wilder rubs his hands together, and his green eyes glint. "Because that's where the fun comes in."

I'm pretty sure the sex is still considered fun, but I don't say so. "You want me to run?"

Brody smirks. "Not just run. We want you to fight."

"Fight?" I check. "Like with kicks and punches?"

I remember not long after I'd first arrived here, when I'd kicked Brody in the balls. God, that feels like an absolute lifetime ago now. I'd been so innocent then—naïve—thinking I could somehow win against these men. That was never going to happen. I was always going to be debased and defiled by them. What on Earth had made me believe I was going to be any different than any other girl who'd come before me? None of them had ever made it to the end without tapping out, and I assume they'd all been a hell of a lot more experienced than I was.

"As long as it's not in the balls," Brody replies, clearly sharing my memory.

Wilder moves closer to me. "We want you to fight us like you don't want it. We want you to make us work for it. Run, when you can, but when you can't, we want you to hit and kick and bite and claw, and struggle beneath us until you can't anymore."

A picture of what they want is forming in my mind, and with it comes a frisson of heat between my thighs. I find myself squirming, pressing my legs together to generate more of the pleasurable sensation. My nipples harden, and this time, instead of being ashamed at my body's reactions, I push my shoulders back farther. They notice, and the hunger in all of their eyes deepens.

To my surprise, I discover I'm no longer frightened...anticipatory, maybe, but I'm not scared of these men. They might push me to my limits, and what they inflict on me might even hurt, but it'll also challenge me, and I will hurt them back. Fighting them will feel good, cathartic. I bite back a smile. I feel as though I'm growing as a person in their presence. I'm growing as a *woman*. The scared girl I was when I arrived here is gradually being left behind, and I'm becoming the type of woman who can handle four intimidating but complicated men.

"I can do that," I tell them.

Wilder sweeps a stray hair that's escaped my ponytail away from my face. "I'm looking forward to it."

"Here you go," Rafferty says without any niceties, as he hands me the small backpack I know will be filled with essentials.

He also gives me a map. I look at it in surprise because I didn't think we were doing the thing where I get the chance to not have to have lots of hot sex with the men. The thing where if I find the hidden present, I get the day off.

"Is this a map to one of the hidden treasures?" I ask, confused.

"Nope. But it is a map of the island. You need to know where you're going, after all. We're going to give you a good head start today. You'll have forty-five minutes before we set off after you."

It seems like a long time.

Rafferty takes my chin firmly between his thumb and forefinger. "We are giving you the extra time because once we catch you, it is going to be wild."

His words of warning don't have the same effect they would have even two days ago. My attraction to these men now, despite the way they've treated me, is too deep. I want to get caught. It should terrify me, and it does to a degree, because it means I'm losing myself in this, and in them. It's going to hurt all the more when they throw me away when my time here is up.

I take the map and shove it in the front pocket of the backpack, zip it closed, and hoist it over my arms, securing it. I give the four men watching me a small wave and, somewhat self-consciously, set off out the door.

As soon as I hit the path, I take a jog onto the beach and start from there. I have no destination now because I have no prize. There's nothing I can claim that will stop this game anymore. From now on, if I get caught, I must have sex with them.

But I'll have to fight them first.

I have my safeword, but that's all that's really left to me, and, as far as I'm aware, only one of the four men even knows what it is.

I wipe my brow. Damn, today is hot. In fact, it's the hottest day since I've been here, and the weather is somewhat warmer than it normally is off the coast of mid-California. It almost feels subtropical, reminiscent of somewhere like Florida. As I keep jogging, a film of sweat covers me, and I need to stop and take a drink. I take the map out of the backpack as I gulp down some water and have a good look.

I could really do with finding a shaded route. I'm going to end up seriously dehydrated otherwise.

As I study the map, I see that if I turn inland, I can take the path through the woods. It is less direct to get where I've decided to head but cooler. The cave I hid out in before is my destination today.

If I can get to the cave, I can keep out of the heat of the day, have a snack, have some water, and think about where to go next.

Part of me just wants to let them catch me now. However, they've already made it clear to me that they need this. Asher especially. The chase is part of this for them, and I don't want to ruin that.

So, on I push, through the heat, jogging as fast as I can without starting to feel unwell. A trickle of sweat runs down my spine, and perspiration prickles across my upper lip and forehead. I'm glad to have my hair pulled well away from my neck. If the guys preferred for me to wear it down, I'd be dying.

BRUTAL LIMITS

I pause on a rocky outcropping to admire the view. There's a gap in the trees, and, between them, the blue of the ocean meets the cloudless sky. Even though I have four men chasing me, I take a moment to draw in a deep breath of clean air and let my eyes slip shut, the sun warming my shoulders. Birds tweet and twitter all around me, and insects buzz as they flit from flower to flower.

God, it's beautiful here. Something settles in my soul, and it dawns on me that I'm at peace.

I can't remember the last time I felt this way. It was before Don came into my life; I know that much.

I dare to allow myself a fantasy where the men accept me for who I am, and I'm allowed to stay. Would I ever be enough for them? I think how many women must have come before me, and my stomach knots. Of course I won't be. I'm surprised they're not bored with me already. Why would they want me to stay when all I've done is lie to them and cause fights? With their looks and money, they can literally have as many women here as they want. I'm a nothing, a nobody.

My sense of peace deserts me, and I turn away from the view. I adjust the backpack on my shoulders and keep going, following the map. A few things look familiar—the stump of a tree, and a certain bush that is growing across the makeshift path. I'm sure I'm on the right route.

I assume a good forty-five minutes has passed by now, and so the men will be on their way.

Remembering my promise to them to give them what they want, I pick up my pace. I'm tried now, however, the heat of the day getting to me, sapping my strength. I want to give myself enough time in the cool confines of the cave to rest and regroup before I set off again.

I'm almost there.

A surge of triumph rises within me when I see the cave. It might be silly because there's only myself here to witness my moment of glory, but I know I did this, that once again I avoided them for long enough to reach my goal. In my own small way, I beat them again because this was my aim, and here I am.

I take the backpack off and stretch in relief because in this heat it feels like it weighs an absolute ton. I step into the cave, and the cool, damp air greets me. I breathe it in, enjoying the freshness after the cloying humidity. I find a comfortable place to sit and flop onto the ground cross-legged, as I rummage through the backpack.

I take a second bottle of water out of the backpack and start to drink that, too. There are only three bottles in here, and none of them are big. I understand why, because it would be hard for me to carry three large bottles of water. It does give me pause for a moment, though. If I were to get lost, or something happened to the men, and I was stuck out here, how would I get water? Of course, I'd be able to find my way back to the hotel...unless I was injured.

I tell myself firmly to stop freaking myself out.

Sometimes when I'm on the run out here and all alone, I get a sense of dread. It's as if there's something stalking me, something that I can't name. I feel it growing nearer all the time, but I don't know why I'm getting such ridiculous premonitions.

Perhaps it's the place.

It's really lonely on this island when you're miles away from anybody else. There's always something of a breeze, too, and sometimes it can stir itself up into a strong wind. The sound of it moaning around the compound one night had kept me awake for hours.

I shiver and wrap my arms around my knees. I don't need to think thoughts like this, I tell myself. I'm safe here in the cave, and I'm sure they are tracking me as we speak.

I snack on one of the energy bars they've helpfully provided me with and sip a little more water. I take it easy, though, not wanting to finish the second bottle and leave myself with only one.

I'm tired from the heat of the day, and I decide to lie down and rest my head on my backpack for five minutes.

Birdsong and the distant crash of the waves are like a lullaby. My thoughts drift, becoming fragmented and muddled...

I awake with a jerk. A noise outside must have woken me. My heart is pounding far too fast, and my mouth is dry. Shit. I must have fallen asleep. That wasn't part of the plan.

I push myself up onto my elbow and peer out of the entrance.

I can't see any of the men. Could there be someone else here?

We are on an island, so I'm sure there won't be anything like cougars around here, thank God. The rustling comes again, and I clutch the backpack closer. Not that it can protect me if there really is something out there.

Then there comes the sound of something heavier. It's a footstep. A booted footstep, to be exact.

Unbidden, the image of my stepfather's face jumps into my mind. My heart lurches into my throat. No, it won't be him. There's no way he'd have found me on the island, and even if he has, the chances of him tracking me to this cave would be pretty remote. If he has found me, I know the guys will be right behind. If they found me with Don, what would they do? Would they just let him take me, or would they fight for me? I liked to think it would be the latter, but perhaps they'd think it was none of their business and hand me over. I can't imagine Rafferty being pleased about the idea of someone coming onto the island without his permission, but he'd also not want any trouble. With Don being a detective, the one thing he's capable of is causing trouble for others. Rafferty might decide it's easier just to let Don take me.

Tears fill my eyes. They're partially from fear, but also sadness at the thought of none of them wanting to fight for me. I hate the way my heart works. No matter how much I try to convince myself this is a business transaction, I can't help but want them to care for me.

The sun is blocked from the entrance as a large figure bends down to peer in. "Well, hello there, Pan."

I exhale a breath of relief, but only partially so. It might not be Don, but it's the next best—or worst—thing.

Trust it to be Brody, the one who still hates me.

"I guess the others aren't here yet. It seems like it's you and me for a little bit of fun time."

I remember Rafferty's words when he promised me that there wouldn't be any one-on-one time with the guys when we played this way. For my safety.

I've realized something. Rafferty is going to be pissed when he finds out what happened between myself and Asher. I'm supposed to only play with the four of them when they're all together so that if it gets too much, I can give Rafferty the secret safeword.

"We ought to wait for the others," I say.

Brody takes three menacing steps toward me. "You don't get to set the rules here, though, Pan. Do you?"

"I know what Rafferty told me," I say, trying to keep my voice calm. "We need to wait for them to get here."

He lunges forward and grabs hold of my ponytail, pulling it to one side. My head twists along with my hair, making my scalp sting. I give a yelp of surprise as he leads me out of the cave that way.

The sun hits my eyes and blinds me for a moment as I blink.

"Get on your knees, bitch," Brody snarls.

He uses my hair to drag me down to the ground. I scramble to kneel, trying to do so without hurting my knees on the rough, pebble covered earth. God, will these men ever stop treating me this way? I just think that I've made a breakthrough, and then something like this happens.

I glare up at him, for once not scared but angry. What's the worst he can do? After all, the only person who's made me bleed here is a woman.

"Keep looking at me like you hate me, Pandora. I dare you."

"I'm not scared of you," I tell him.

"You ought to be," he says, voice low as he leans close.

I remember what they told me about making them work for it. Now seems the perfect time to do what they asked. I look left and right, trying to judge the best route for my escape. If I go right, I might bang straight into the others. I can't decide if that's a good or bad thing.

"Damn, Brody's first."

The sound of Asher's voice has me sucking in air in relief. I never thought I'd have that reaction to hearing Asher bearing down on me. I know what direction they're coming from now, so I can run the opposite way. That's not the only reason I'm relieved, however.

Right now, I think out of all these men, Brody is the one who could actually be a real danger to me.

There's something within him that is so angry at me, and I don't understand why.

Brody gives me a nasty smirk and keeps holding on to my hair.

I brace myself. There's rustling in the bushes as the others approach. Brody's attention is diverted by it, too, and I take the opportunity. I reach up to where his hand is gripped around my ponytail and yank it away, then I'm on my feet, as though I'm a sprinter on a starting block, and I'm running.

"What the fuck!" Brody yells after me.

I no longer have my backpack. I left it in the cave, which means I also no longer have any water or the map. I tell myself it doesn't matter, that the men will catch me soon, but it still unnerves me.

I keep going. Behind me comes the crash of large bodies running through the undergrowth, and I recognize the shouts of the men. Rafferty, Wilder, Asher, and Brody. All four are on my tail now. Will they be angry with Brody for getting ahead

BRUTAL LIMITS 161

of them and then letting me get away, or was this all part of the plan?

I'm unsure where I'm going. Low-lying branches and brambles lash against my legs, and I'm grateful for the material of my pants. It's hot, though, and the run only makes me hotter. My cheeks burn, and fresh sweat trickles between my breasts and into my bra. Though I know they want me to run, I'm not sure how much longer I can keep going.

The sounds of them behind me grow louder. They're gaining on me. I risk a glance over my shoulder and catch a glimpse of tattooed skin and a form-fitting t-shirt. Wilder. As the biggest of them all, he's got the longest legs, and I'm guessing the undergrowth doesn't pose much of an issue for him. He must just flatten it as he goes.

I've slowed—and subconsciously, I might have done so on purpose. Thick forearms wrap around my waist from behind and haul me off my feet. I shriek and kick, but my feet only meet air.

"Gotcha," Wilder says against my ear.

I remember my role in all this, and I continue to struggle. The others catch up, and I'm pleased to see I'm not the only one who's out of breath.

Brody comes to stand in front of me, and I kick out at him. He grabs both my ankles and then laughs as he forces my calves around his hips. He moves closer to Wilder, so I'm crushed between them.

"Not going anywhere now," he says.

My hands are pinned to my sides by Wilder's arms.

Brody smirks. "Keep struggling. You're making me hard."

I don't know where I get it from, but I manage to summon some saliva from somewhere, and, without even thinking, I spit in Brody's face. It hits his cheek, and I gasp, realizing what I've done. I half expect him to slap me in return, but instead, he lets go of one of my ankles and reaches up to wipe my spit from his face. Instead of using his t-shirt to clean it away, he puts his fingers in his mouth, licking my saliva from them.

"I hope there's more of that to come," he says. "Wilder, let go a moment."

Strong arms release me for a second.

Brody reaches out and grabs the bottom of my tank top then rips it, tearing it right to the neck. The material flaps open, exposing my bra and sweaty skin. Then I'm once more clamped in Wilder's arms, and Brody leans in and runs his tongue between my cleavage, lapping up the salty sweat.

The man is a complete freak.

Asher stands, panting slightly, with his hands on his hips as he looks around. "We're going to need somewhere a bit more comfortable for today's fun," he says.

Rafferty imitates Asher's hands on hips stance as he gets his breath back.

He glances at the uneven ground and frowns. "How about we head to the beach?" he suggests. "It won't be comfortable for Honor if we carry out our plans for today here."

"Just what I was saying," Asher replies.

"Who gives a fuck if she's comfortable?" Brody scowls.

"I'm not fucking on this ground." Asher pushes Brody in the shoulder. "Do you want splinters in your hands and gravel stuck in your knees? It's full of debris and crap from people who've tried to make fires and shelter around here when we ran wilderness weekends. Don't be a dick."

Brody doesn't answer, but his dark scowl deepens.

The next moment, Wilder turns me around and sweeps me up into his arms, making my head spin. I continue to struggle, but he's so much bigger than I am, I don't stand a chance.

He carries me through the undergrowth like a giant out of a fairy story. Though I know I'm supposed to fight, I fall still for a moment. I need to conserve my energy for what's coming next. I wrap my arms around his neck and rest my head against his chest. For all his size, and his scary persona, Wilder is the one who makes me feel the safest.

When he reaches the beach, he sets me down on the sand and gives me a grin of such intensity that it takes my breath away.

I glance either side of me, wondering if I should try to run again, but the sand is impossibly soft and my feet will sink right into it, making it difficult. Besides, they've caught me now. I guess this is where they're going to want me to fight.

"Today is going to be next level, Snow," Wilder warns. The others are bringing up the rear, still talking and out of view. "We need this, though. All of us. Maybe you do, too. Do what we want, take us well, and we'll reward you."

He strokes his finger down my cheek, and I shiver.

Take what, exactly? Just what do they have planned for me?

Chapter Sixteen
Honor

THE SUN MIGHT AS WELL have gone behind a cloud for all the warmth I feel as the three men join us.

"Strip," Rafferty orders as he strolls onto the sand.

I swallow hard, still not used to the way the four of them watch me so predatorily. My tank is already hanging open, and barely staying on my shoulders, but I remember my part in this.

I'm defiant. "No."

"You want us to tear the rest of your clothes from your body?"

I scowl, but the expression is fake. A tingling has already tightened my core and my nipples are hard, despite the warm day.

Wilder is closest to me. Without giving me the option to change my mind, he yanks the remains of my top from my arms and unclips my bra in what is practically a professional move. He whips it away from me and throws it to the sand, so I'm standing there, bare-breasted.

Instead of covering myself up, I put back my shoulders and lift my chin.

"I still can't figure out how such a tiny thing like you grew such a juicy pair," Asher says.

And...we're back to the degradation.

He comes and stands behind me and reaches around my front where he uses the thumb and finger of each hand to pull my nipples so hard, I let out a small yelp. It feels good, sending sparks to my core, but I remember my role. I try to slap his hands away and when that doesn't work, I deliver a swift elbow to his chest.

"Bitch," he says, though there's a smile in his words. "Someone hold her still."

Wilder grabs both my arms and holds them above my head, so I'm in much the same position as I'd been when they'd cuffed me to the rings in the bunker. It gives Asher unfettered access to my tits, and he twists and pulls at my nipples until they're red and distended. My pussy grows wet, and I wind my hips, desperate for attention there.

I whimper and hang my head. I'm supposed to be fighting them, but right now I'd given anything for one of them to fuck me already.

"Goddamn, look at those tits," Brody says, rubbing the outline of his cock.

Asher plumps my breasts and pushes them up and together like an offering to the other men.

Rafferty takes that offer and moves in closer. He ducks his head and sucks both my nipples into his mouth as Asher holds the weight of my breasts for him. There's something utterly obscene about it, and yet it still turns me on, because it seems I'm messed up in the head that way.

"Imagine if we knocked her up," Brody says with a nasty sneer. "We could all take turns drinking some titty juice."

I can't say anything in response to his deliberate degrading comments because this is what is signed up for, and I can't move, but despite the pleasure Asher and Rafferty are eliciting in me, I still manage to throw Brody a hateful glare.

"Keep that up, Pandora, and you'll really regret it. I've warned you." Brody glares right back at me.

Rafferty lets go of my nipples with an obscene pop of his mouth. Asher continues to maul my breasts as Rafferty unzips the large backpack he has been carrying and takes out a huge blanket, which he spreads out beneath a tree on the edge of the sand to give us some shade.

For one crazy moment, I wonder if we're going to have a picnic, but then I realize the only thing being eaten will be me.

Wilder releases my arms, picks me up, and places me down on the blanket with a level of care I have come to expect from the one I see as somewhat of a gentle giant. The moment he lets go of me, I flip onto all fours and try to crawl away.

"Uh-uh," Wilder says. "No, you don't."

He grabs my leg and yanks me back down again, flipping me over so I'm lying on my back. I'm naked from the waist up, but I won't be for long.

As if they have one hive mind they share, the men surround me, pinning me down between them. Brody has my left arm, Asher my right. Wilder and Rafferty are at my lower half, tugging off my boots and socks and then working on my pants and panties.

"Get off me," I cry, though I don't mean it for a second.

"Not a chance," Rafferty replies. "You're all ours now."

I wriggle and kick out at them, just the way they've asked, but they're far too strong for me. Not even a minute has passed before I'm complete naked.

They release me, but there's no point in trying to run. They're surrounding me, and there's nowhere I can go. Besides, I'm slippery between my thighs and my breasts are full and aching. I want their touch, even if I'm going to make them work for it.

The four men begin to undress at the same time. They make quick work of it, too. Soon, I am faced by four naked men, all of them hard. They are all impressive in their own way, but every time I see Wilder naked I get a little frisson of fear mixed in with the thrill. The metal of his piercing catches the sunlight. He's s altogether too much.

"We have a new rule for today, Snow." Wilder stares down at me, casually running his hand up and down his length as he speaks.

"And what might that be?" I ask.

"No condoms. And us, one after the other." Brody answers this time and gives me an intense stare, daring me to object.

He watches me like a hawk, and I know he's waiting for me to say the words *no, stop, I can't*. I glance at Rafferty to see the same expectation in his gaze, except that he doesn't seem to feel any triumph, more a detached curiosity as to just how far I will go.

"We are all clean, Snow," Wilder says. "We've always used condoms with any woman who comes here. We also take full health tests after."

"That's an awful lot of trust you're asking me to have in you all," I point out.

"It is, isn't it?" Brody replies. "Almost, one might say, a million dollars' worth of trust."

He's got me there.

"I want to slide in you and feel all of that cum" Rafferty says.

I know how he gets off on that kind of thing. I bet he's the fucker who suggested this. Just as I was thinking he was my favorite of the bunch.

Call me crazy, but I do believe them about being clean. The reason I believe them is Rafferty. He's a stickler for his rules and regulations, and we have a signed contract. I doubt he'd okay this if he thought any communicable diseases were about to be spread around.

I glance at him furtively, and he's calm and collected.

"It's been two days since you started the pill. As long as you've been taking it the same time each day, you won't have to worry."

I have been.

In some ways, this is way less bad than I thought it might be. Sex, no matter how much they throw at me, I seem to be able to cope with. Isolation. Degradation. Pain. Those things I fear more. I have a couple of days left, and I get the money, and this seems an easy way to get it. After all, how hard can it be? I agree before I can change my mind.

"Okay. No condoms."

God, I must be absolutely crazy.

"Get her ready," Rafferty orders Brody.

Brody drops to his knees and crawls between my legs. He pushes me down until I'm splayed out fully on the blanket, with my legs spread up and to the side. Then he eats me as if I am a Michelin-starred menu all laid out for him.

For a man who seems to hate me, he sure seems to like the taste of me.

It doesn't take long before I'm almost delirious from the pleasure and torture his tongue is giving me. He curls it around my clit and sucks and licks with exactly the right amount of pressure. He pushes two fingers inside me and pumps them in rhythm to that clever tongue of his.

The build-up I've been experiencing ever since I stood in front of them first thing that morning is finally reaching its peak. I'm a clenched ball of desire and arousal, and all I want is to topple over the edge.

I start to come, and as I cry out and convulse, he pulls his mouth away, slides up my body in one smooth motion, and thrusts deep inside me. He fills me as I'm still contracting.

I scream at the intensity of it.

"Oh, fuck. Oh, God. Oh, fuck."

My back arches and my pussy clamps around his cock, but Brody holds still inside me. He lets me shake and shudder around him, and then he leans in and speaks low and hot against my ear.

"Remember you're supposed to fight me."

I had forgotten. His words bring me back to the game, and even though I want to be fucked, I lift my hands and pummel at his shoulders. He grabs them and pins my wrists down to the blanket above my head. I squirm and wriggle beneath him and manage to get one hand free. I scratch his back before he grabs my wrist again and pins it back with the other.

This whole time, his cock is like iron inside me, and God, it feels good.

With my hands pinned, he moves inside me, thrusting hard. His expression is contorted as he fucks me. I remember I can use my teeth, so I turn my head to sink them into his strong bicep.

"Ahh, bitch." He sucks air in over his teeth and rams into me even harder.

I take pleasure in seeing my teeth marks in small red indentations in his tan skin.

The others are still standing by, all erect. I catch Rafferty's eye, and he gives me a small nod. It's his way of telling me that he remembers my safeword. That no matter what happens, he can make this whole thing stop.

"No, no," I moan. "Please, stop."

"Shut it," Brody snaps.

He manages to get both my wrists in one of his hands and he clamps his other palm across my mouth. I can no longer say the safeword, even if I wanted to—which I don't—and for some reason it takes my arousal up another level.

Brody's hips slam into me, faster and faster, his breathing hot and heavy. My second orgasm crests, and I know I'm going to come again.

This whole thing is so intense. My eyes roll and toes curl. The sensation is overwhelming. The skin all over my body tingles in over-sensitized pleasure. My nipples are hard and pointed, and all the tiny hairs on the back of my neck are standing on end.

I slowly come down as Brody grunts while he thrusts deeper and deeper inside of me.

Suddenly, he pulls out of my pussy and stands.

What the hell is wrong? I thought they were going to take this in turns. Why hasn't he come?

Rafferty moves into position between my legs, bracing himself above me, and then he's sinking into me, filling the spot that Brody left empty.

Rafferty feels amazing, but I'm still confused as to why Brody didn't come. I look at him to check, and nope, still as hard as ever.

Rafferty thrusts five, six times, and then he pulls out, too.

This time it's Asher who falls on me like a starving man. He fucks into me like an animal, jerking his hips hard as he slams into me repeatedly. Then he pulls off me, too.

"Your turn, big boy," Asher says to Wilder.

Wilder approaches me slowly, as if he's got all day. He holds his big bulk above me, the massive column of his arms taking his weight.

"Hey," he says to me, pushing my sweaty hair out of my face.

"Hey," I say back, my voice almost a whisper.

Carefully but inexorably, he pushes his way inside me.

Despite having done this before, the burn of the stretch still takes my breath away. He's thick and heavy, the weight of him filling my pussy completely.

When he's balls deep, he lifts up and gives me smile, and then he leans down and licks a long stripe over my throat before biting at my jaw and taking my mouth in a heated kiss as he begins to move.

Holy mother of God, that piercing of his is hitting me in the exact place I need it.

Another orgasm builds, and shame at the way my body is betraying me by making me come repeatedly for these men fills me.

"You want it, so don't fight it, Snow." Wilder breaks off the kiss to speak. "I want you to come for me. It's so beautiful."

I don't think I'll be able to stop it, even if I tried. His piercing is hitting my g-spot repeatedly, and I'm seeing stars.

As I give up the fight and fall over the edge, he swears under his breath, and his hips fall still. His massive cock twitches inside me, and he shoots his hot load into me.

Without the condom, I can feel every thick jet as it fills me up.

He pulls out of me and grabs my ankles, holding my legs up in the air.

What the actual fuck? I struggle, but he holds me firm.

"Let's keep all this in place for Rafferty, shall we?" he says with a wink.

This is the most debased I think I've ever been.

The word is on the tip of my tongue. I look over at Rafferty as I remain hoisted in the air like some piece of meat. Then I think of the money. And, if I'm being truthful, I also think of the other orgasms I'm probably going to have any minute now.

Orgasms and money for a little shame. It's not a bad deal.

Rafferty walks over slowly, and as Wilder lowers my legs and spreads them for his friend, he fills me immediately with his dick.

"Christ, she's a sloppy mess," he says. "A guy could get a complex going after you, Wilder."

If I thought there was any camaraderie between us all after the movie last night, my naïve fantasies are shattered. The camaraderie is all for them, and I'm just the toy once again.

Rafferty fucks me hard and fast, and when he comes, it's with a shout, not a grunt, as he spills deep inside me. When he pulls out, Wilder does his sick little trick again. He gives me a lewd wink. I turn my face away, not wanting to look at him.

Next is Brody, and I kind of switch off at this point. He fucks me the hardest so far, and that's no surprise. He's probably taking his hate out on me, in some sort of sick and twisted way.

I can't quite believe it's happening, and in some ways wish it wasn't. I don't want to be an active participant in this anymore, not with Asher sneering from my right, and Wilder, the one I thought cared, staring with his dick half hard again at my left. My body has other ideas, however.

It's not unpleasant. I'm still enjoying the sensations, but my mind is drifted elsewhere.

Brody comes with a deep groan, and he collapses on me for a moment, sweaty skin against sweaty skin as we swelter despite the shade due to the strenuous activity.

"That's a good girl, Pandora. You take it so beautifully." He kisses my cheek, and I stare at him as I wipe it away.

He laughs and shakes his head as he walks off.

Wilder goes to lift my legs again, but Asher is already there, settling between them.

"God you're so full of us," he says.

He isn't degrading me the way the others have, even Wilder. His voice holds an element of awe to it.

He looks down at me as if I'm a wondrous being. "You make all of our dreams come true, don't you?"

He snaps his hips and groans, and I am caught up in it once again. The way he's looking at me as if I am a rare, precious thing, not their debased toy. The way he's hitting the right spots. He works me like an animal, and every time he hits deep, he grinds himself against my clit, giving me the sensations I need to find myself climbing for yet another orgasm.

Asher puts his hand around my throat and squeezes. Before now, I would have panicked, but I don't. I embrace the sensation of the amount of oxygen reducing in my brain, the dreamy quality it gives me. Every feeling in my body is somehow heightened, and now that I'm not ruled by fear, I can appreciate it. It clearly turns Asher on, too, his expression intense.

I trust him now, I realize. He won't hurt me.

Asher sucks one sore nipple into his mouth and soothes it with his tongue, and I fall over the edge, my legs wrapping around him as I come so hard, I whimper. He comes, too, and fills me with my fourth load of the day.

I'm covered in sweat, and cum is oozing from between my legs. I feel filthy and debauched, and all I want to do right now is go back to the house and have a shower.

At least it's over...for now.

When I open my eyes, though, Wilder's there again, fully erect once more.

Oh, no, no way. I can't take him again, surely?

"They've all stretched you out for me, Snow. You need it a little bit more, though." His words sound tortured, his voice thick. "I need you to be a good girl and let me stretch you out with my big cock."

This is his thing, right? Rafferty's thing is watching them all take me, and this is Wilder's.

Wilder kneels between my legs, but he doesn't slide into me. Instead, he flips me over so I am on my hands and knees. He spreads my ass cheeks apart.

"Look at all this dripping out of her." He sweeps a finger through my folds, playing in the thick creamy liquid there.

I'm literally dripping, and it's utterly humiliating.

Wilder hoists my ass higher in the air, so the men can get a good look at my pussy filled with them, and then he slowly pushes inside of me.

When he starts to move, the squelching sounds make my cheeks heat.

I don't think I can come again, so I really do turn into his precious toy and just let him use me. Wilder, though, has different ideas. He reaches around and finds my clit. He presses two thick fingers either side of it and traps my clit between them. He starts to rhythmically squeeze his fingers together and apart. Having my clit squeezed this way is a new sensation, and at first it feels too overwhelming and raw, but as he keeps it up, the squeezing, along with his deep thrusts, has me climbing that hill to oblivion once more.

"So fucking perfect and beautiful for us," Wilder whispers in my ear. "You're the best we ever had, Snow, and I'll never find anyone like you."

His words are just for me, not loud enough for the others to hear, and he kisses me on the ear as I fall over the edge with a loud cry and come so hard, I lose all strength. I fall forward onto the blanket, my vision blurry.

"Jesus, Wilder, you fucked her unconscious," Brody says with a laugh.

Wilder pulls out and turns me over and looks at me with concern in his gaze. "Are you okay, Snow?" he asks seriously.

I can't answer him because I'm such a hot, sticky, boneless mess that I've lost all power of speech.

"You did so good," he says softly.

He kisses my forehead as if I'm someone precious to him. Not a cum covered slut that they're all using as the butt of their jokes.

"Let's get you cleaned up," he says.

Wilder picks me up and carries me out from the shade and down the beach with him, followed by Rafferty.

As we reach the ocean, he wades in. The cold is shocking after I've been so hot, but it feels amazing. He wades deeper until the water is lapping around his shoulders and over me, too, soothing my sore places, and bathes me.

This is such a head fuck.

Right now, like this, I feel so cherished and cared for. Then the switch will flip again, and they'll use me the way they do.

I realize something. I've enjoyed it, too, haven't I? It's me framing it this way. Not them. They say stuff to me that is degrading, yes, but I could say stuff back. I just don't.

It's a game to them. A sex game, and when the games are over, they don't treat me that way, and even when they do, they make sure I come. Every time.

I test something out.

"I'll still need a shower when I get in. You guys come a lot." I smile up at Wilder. "Except for Brody." Then I wiggle my little finger with a wink.

Brody scowls, but to my delight, the other three crack up laughing, and Asher wiggles his little finger, too. Brody pushes him over into the ocean, and they start a play fight, splashing and dunking each other under the water.

Maybe, my whole hang-up about me being a fuck toy is because of my own mind set?

Can I change it? That's the question.

Chapter Seventeen
Brody

IT'S EVENING NOW. THE sun has set, and the mood is light. Honor is having a soak in the bath, which I guess she earned. Wilder has the firepit going, and we're going to grill outside. It's still warm, but the breeze has picked up, providing some cooler moments.

I sip at my beer, sitting slightly away from the others.

I've had an uncomfortable thought today, and now I've had it, I can't shake it. The three of them are all starting to fall for Honor to some degree or another. They might deny it, but they are. The headfuck is Asher. When the hell did he care about anyone or anything? The only one who still has his head screwed on right is Rafferty, but even he seems to be increasingly swayed by Honor and her fucking magic pussy.

The four of us were always so tight, we knew no woman would ever come between us. It's what made it feel safe to play the way we have. Now, Honor is changing that. Give it a few more days, and honestly? If my brothers had to choose, her or me, I'm not sure which way they'd fall.

It fucking hurts. It takes me forever to trust. First, Pastor Wren fucked me up, and then the military finished the job.

These men were my safe haven. My brothers in vengeance. And now they're all having their heads turned by what? Some pussy. That's all she is at the end of the day.

Part of me wants her gone. Another part of me, a tiny, deep part of me I barely want to acknowledge, never wants her to leave. Even feeling like this, angry, in turmoil, I still feel more alive than I have in a long time. If she goes, everything will feel cold, empty again.

Fuck. I put the beer to one side, needing something stronger.

Getting up, I head to the bar in the corner of the pool area and pour myself a large shot of whisky. I sip it as I head back to the chair I've chosen.

As I sit once more, Honor walks out of the double doors. I stare at her, and that little something in me, that tiny spark, expands.

She's wearing a long, red dress. It's floaty, and the breeze plays with it as she walks toward the other three men. Her hair is down in loose, tumbling waves, and she's wearing red lipstick to match the dress. She looks like something from a painting; she's that beautiful.

I sip the whisky and watch as Asher turns first, seeing her. His eyes hold a thousand emotions as he watches her approach.

Yeah, this girl is going to fuck everything up.

All of it.

It hasn't escaped my notice that no one has even asked what our next steps are with Pastor Wren. We had a lead on him, but we've been far from focused when it comes to following it through. Asher has been more concerned with locating Honor's stepfather than he has nailing down Wren.

We're all way too distracted, but, looking at her now, how could anyone blame us?

The breeze plays with her dress once more, but it's not much of a breeze. In fact, there's an odd stillness to everything tonight. As if the Earth is pausing and holding its breath. I don't know what it means, only that I feel it.

Honor sits next to Asher and smiles as he offers her a glass of wine.

She can't stay. It wouldn't work. Four men can share a woman when it is just sex, but not if it becomes something more. Once feelings get involved, then possessiveness becomes an issue. We will start fighting among ourselves. It's absolutely what will happen. There's no other outcome. We've never had jealousy between us, and I don't want it to start now.

Tomorrow's game needs to break her. I will push her so far she fucking ends this. I can't openly force her to leave, or they will all hate me, but if I push her so much she cannot take anymore, then *she* will end this. Then things can go back to normal.

I just need to find something that works. With Honor, I think the humiliation is the thing she can't deal with. The degradation. So that's what I will throw at her in spades. It's not my kink. I'll use it as a weapon against her, though.

Rafferty tosses a couple of steaks onto the grill, and the scent of sizzling meat fills the air. I squeeze my eyes shut and try not to let it take me back to my time in Iraq.

I fail.

Without saying anything, I get to my feet and put some distance between myself and the cooking meat. The underwater lights are on in the pool, and the water shimmers.

Overhead, a tiny bat ducks and dives, chasing some insect that's too small for my eyes to see.

I stand with my back to the others and gulp down the rest of my drink.

Movement comes beside me, and I glance down to find Honor standing there.

"Are you okay?" she asks.

Immediately, I go on the defensive. "Why are you asking me that?"

"Because I noticed you went pale and then came over here. I was worried about you."

Men don't do shit like this. My buddies and I never ask how we're doing. At the most, you might get a punch in the shoulder and get ribbed. Taking the piss was an easier way of dealing with things than actually dealing with things.

"I'm fine. I just don't like the smell of meat cooking."

"Is that why you're a vegetarian—or is it pescatarian?"

So, she's noticed that, too. What else has she learned about us during her time here? Is it possible that she actually knows far more about us than we do about her? But no, she doesn't know about Wren. She doesn't know what brought us all together. She might think she does, but she won't have any details. That sort of shit is not the sort you share.

"Pescatarian," I admit. "Fish doesn't affect me the same way."

"Is it because of your time in the army?"

I snap. "It's none of your business, Pan."

She shrinks a little, and I immediately feel bad. I force myself to shake it off. I can't fall for this girl. *I can't, I can't, I can't.*

I'm relieved when Rafferty calls us over to eat. He's done a selection of food to cater to us all—rare steak for the carnivores, a barbequed white seabass fillet for me, and veggie skewers and fresh bread for Asher. Everyone else is in a jovial mood, laughing and chatting. The only one who has the black cloud hanging over him is me. Why am I the only one who can see what'll happen to us if we let this continue?

Fuck. Maybe it's already too late. What will happen even if I do manage to force her to quit? This sense of celebration will abandon us, and we'll be back to focusing on Wren. We'll go back to being unhappy and intense.

It's what has to be done, though, even if it might hurt in the short term.

The others all eat and drink with gusto, but I pick at my fish. It's perfectly grilled and fresh from the sea, but I can barely taste it.

The staff arrive to clear up after us—one benefit of living in a resort—and we take our drinks to the fire pit. Honor's cheeks are pink, and her eyes glowing. She's so beautiful it physically hurts my chest, and from the way the others are all looking at her, I can tell they feel the same way. They're all jostling for her attention, trying to be the ones who get to sit next to her, or refill her wine glass, or make her laugh.

It's been a long, full-on day, and the combination of the day's sun, sex, full stomachs, and alcohol soon makes everyone drowsy.

A quiet settles over us.

"We could do with some music," Rafferty says. "Anyone bring their phone?"

No one has.

Wilder picks up an empty tub that had some of the salad fixings in it and turns it upside down, and using it as drum, hammers out a steady beat. He sings, not too shabbily, a couple of songs, and on the second one, Asher joins in, too. Then there's silence once more. I think I'll go grab my iPhone and put some music on.

From out of nowhere, a sweet voice fills the air, singing a song I don't recognize.

A hush settles over us, our combined breath caught in awe.

Honor's eyes are shut as she sings, and it's as though she's transported to another place. Her voice rises and swells, and the hairs lift on the back of my neck and goosebumps prickle across my forearms. My heart clenches.

Jesus Christ. Her voice is beautiful.

The song comes to an end, and she falls quiet. Her eyes are open, but she glances to the ground and takes another swig of her wine, as though she'd forgotten herself for a moment and is now embarrassed.

"Fucking hell, Snow," Wilder says. "Where have you been hiding that voice?"

She shrugs. "Nowhere, really. Guess I just haven't been in a singing mood until now."

"What song was that?" Rafferty asks. "I didn't recognize it."

Her embarrassment seems to deepen. "No, you wouldn't. It was one of mine."

Rafferty raises an eyebrow. "One of your songs? You mean, you wrote it?"

She nods.

"Wow, princess. You could go far with that talent. You could be on stage."

"I don't want to be on stage," she admits. "I just want to write songs."

"You want to write songs?" Asher confirms.

"It's a pipe dream, I know."

Wilder offers her a smile. "Dreams can come true."

She doesn't seem convinced. "Can they?"

"We got you, didn't we?"

Her breath catches, and she stares at him.

He shakes his head and drags his hand through his long hair. "Ignore me." He raises his beer bottle. "Booze has loosened my tongue."

But it's too late. The words are already out of his mouth, and we all know exactly what he means. He's saying that Honor is a dream come true for us, and you don't just let dreams walk away from you once you've achieved them.

I put down my glass and stand. "I'm going to bed."

I don't wait for any of them to say goodnight. I turn and stalk back to the building, feeling as though my control of this situation is slipping from my fingers.

Tomorrow, something needs to change.

Chapter Eighteen
Honor

LAST NIGHT FELT DIFFERENT.

The men were finally starting to see me for who I truly was, and, in turn, I was bonding with them, too.

How many days do I have left?

Rafferty told me five days, but we haven't discussed if that included the day we were on, or if it was five days from the following day. Does he mean five active days? As in the days we are doing the hunts. I have had a couple of rest days, and I am pretty sure they don't count? Am I expected to leave on day five, or will they at least give me an extra day to rest and gather my belongings?

The idea of finally leaving, getting my freedom, should have me over the moon. Instead, it leaves me hollow inside.

Oh, my God. I don't want to go. Not really. Not yet. What the hell is wrong with me?

I reason with myself that I won't be able to take much more than a few more days of this, physically, at least. My body will get tired. I'll need to rest. Still, the idea of suddenly being alone and without the company of these men seems strangely melancholy to me.

I try to buoy myself with the thought I could be a mere forty-eight hours from becoming a millionaire. It doesn't feel real at all. Me, Honor, as a millionaire.

The possibilities that kind of money opens up for me are breathtaking. I can go anywhere, and I'll finally have the kind of money that buys private investigators—the best of the bunch. I don't know what they'll find on Don, but I know they'll find enough to prove he's as bent as they come. What I really want is to prove he murdered my mother, but I'll settle for putting him behind bars.

One thing prisoners hate is a cop. They won't make being in jail pleasant for him.

I want to picture myself in my own home, finally safe, but I can't. No matter how I want to imagine myself as a wealthy woman living somewhere Don can never find me, I can't place myself anywhere other than here. Even my dream of finding a villa and settling down in Montenegro has lost its appeal to me now.

A painful lump chokes my throat.

The thought of never seeing any of the guys again brings tears to my eyes. I'll never again be held against Wilder's strong chest. I'll never again feel like everything is under control like I do when I'm with Rafferty. I'll never be on my toes the way I am with Asher. Brody, well, there's more to Brody than the wall he currently has put up against me. He's hurt, and I hurt him even more, and that's on me.

They're bound to want to play again today. Why wouldn't they, when there's such a short time left?

The way they reacted to me singing filled me with a glow of pride. My mom always said I was good, but she's my mother.

Your mother has to support you in such things, right? Mind you, before he became creep of the century, even Don said I had a rare talent. I had put that down to the fact I later discovered he'd been dreaming about getting into my pants, the pervert. Still, he'd said I should go for it and try to write music, and now these men have said the same.

I'll get over these men; I know I will. After all, I don't love them, right? I mean, I can't love them. Who falls in love in a matter of days? Furthermore, who falls in love with people who treat them like a toy? No one. That's who.

I square my shoulders and check my reflection. I've dressed in the same outfit but a clean, non-ripped version of it. There are always more black tank tops, and more skinny fitting trousers, and clean underwear. I reckon these guys have a private side deal with a Lara Croft cos-play costumier. I giggle a little at my own silly joke, and then sober.

Another hunt awaits me. Another depraved game. What will they do this time?

I leave my room in search of the guys.

I find them around the pool, which is new. They glance at me, and in Wilder's gaze there's an affection he rarely hides anymore. Rafferty is, as usual, all business. Asher, I can't read, and wouldn't ever try. He's mercurial and unpredictable. Brody is glowering and brooding, so no change there.

"Here's your map," Rafferty says. "Today is a shorter lead time for you. We suggest you use it wisely."

"Any...erm, instructions?" I ask. Yesterday they wanted me to fight them. What will they ask for today?

"Just run hard and fast, and pray we don't catch you," Asher says with his trademark sneer.

I see through him now, though. At the heart of Asher is a hurt boy.

At the heart of Wilder is a gentle giant. Rafferty is cold, yes, you can't deny that, but he is also responsible, and the one who makes sure things never go too far. Brody? Brody is a man who has a lot of issues, and frankly, it's not my place to psychoanalyze him. He'd hate me for it.

I hit the beach and do as they say, running hard and fast. After a while, I slow down, the sun too ferocious for me to keep up this speed. I'm panting hard, and my throat is parched. Deciding I need to cool down, I take a trail from the beach into the wooded area bordering it. I went a different way today, and I don't know this direction half as well as I know the route to the cave.

Once in the woods, I take my backpack off and remove my top. Who cares? The only things to see me are the birds and the bees and any of the men if they catch me, and they've seen it all before. In just my bra, and in the shade, I begin to cool down.

"Such a slut. You're even half naked when you're alone."

I jump and turn to face Brody, my hand on my chest. "Jesus, Brody, you scared me."

His face is angry, dark, and there's confliction in his gaze. For a terrible moment, I wonder if he's going to hurt me. I saw that look once before, on a boy right before he beat up a smaller kid.

What's Brody conflicted about?

I automatically take a step back.

"You going to run? I'll catch you in a beat."

"Rafferty says—"

"Rafferty says." He mimics my voice, and it's horrible and cruel. "Fucking shut up, dumb bitch. Get on your knees."

"What? No? Rafferty made me promise. No playing unless we're all together."

He cocks his head. "Oh, so, it's perfectly fine for you to break the rules if it's with Asher and Wilder, but not with me."

My stomach knots. He has me there. His comment also makes me realize the guys have been talking about me. It shouldn't come as a surprise that they would, but it still makes me feel icky inside. Was Asher boasting that he got me to fuck him, even after he'd almost killed someone?

My cheeks burn. "That was different. It just happened. I didn't think about the rules at the time, but I am now."

"Because it's me, you mean?" He snorts. "Anyway, I don't have to follow anyone's rules but my own."

My heart misses a few beats. Rafferty will kill him if I tell him of this. Do I want that? I can use it to get Brody to back off, maybe, but it might make him angrier and have the opposite effect.

"I'm not doing this. I won't disobey Rafferty even if you are happy to. Either I carry on running, or we wait for them to catch us up."

"They aren't going to be here for a long while. They went in another direction."

It sinks in then. He's engineered this.

"Brody, what do you want?"

"Get on your fucking knees."

I shake my head. This is not me playing; this is me saying no for real.

He grabs my shoulders and forces me down, then he pulls my ponytail, wraps it around his fist, and starts to walk away. It means I have to crawl after him, if I don't want to get scalped. The backpack swings to the side as I move and is uncomfortable.

He turns and looks down at me. "Let's go find the others, then, shall we? Come on, crawl, bitch."

I try to pull away, but the pain at my scalp makes my eyes sting. Why is he being so vicious?

"Or...you can leave?" he suggests. "Just go. Tell Rafferty you're done. We all know this is still a game. He's not said so, but I know damn well Rafferty has given you an out. It's obvious. He wouldn't risk it otherwise. You wouldn't still be here happily play-acting our slut if you didn't have an out."

"You want me to use the safeword?" I don't deny I have one. What's the point?

"Yes, I do. Say it, take the money you're owed up to now, and fuck off."

His words are cold, and they sink in like a stone.

He turns to me. "Otherwise, I am going to make your life a living hell."

"I could tell them you've pressured me into this," I say.

"You do that, and you're dead."

I don't think he means that. I don't want to risk finding out I'm wrong, though.

There's a rock in front of Brody, and he's focusing on me crawling along behind him. I reach out and grab his ankle, wrong footing him. He trips and lands awkwardly on the boulder, sending him flying. White hot pain shoots through my scalp as he yanks on my hair as he falls. I let out a scream, but thankfully, he loses his grip and lands with a thud.

I glance at him once to make sure he's okay. He is, but he's twisted on the ground, and struggling to get up. I don't hesitate a second longer. I flee.

Hard and fast, I push myself, arms and legs pumping. I don't know where I am going or what I will do to sort this out. I think I am going to have to tell Rafferty something. Maybe that I don't want them chasing me alone anymore. If we have to play as a group, they have to chase me as a group, or I want to finish this. I think he'll agree to it. I don't have to name Brody that way, but simply say I don't feel safe, as if any of the other three catch me alone, I can't guarantee they won't hurt me.

"Honor." Brody's voice comes after me, loud and strained as if he's in pain. I don't stop. Tough.

"Honor, it's not safe that way. There are cliffs. Fuck," he shouts. "Honor, fucking wait. Jesus. I can't run. I've twisted my ankle. You're not safe."

I ignore him and keep moving. He'll say anything right now to get me back there with him so he can carry on his sick games and make me leave.

Screw him. I won't go back and let him win. I will see this out to the end. I'll get my million, and more importantly, I'll get to leave on my terms and the other three's terms, not Brody's.

He doesn't get to send me away and decide how this ends for the rest of us.

Adrenaline fuels me to keep pushing on and forward. I run faster than I have before, despite the heat. After a while, I slow to more of a jog, lungs burning, but I still don't stop.

Eventually, I need to have a drink. I take the water out of my backpack, alert to Brody following me, but I can't hear him. After having half the bottle of water, I take out the map and try to get my bearings so I can double back and head to the resort. The men will find me there eventually.

I frown as I look at the map. I can figure out roughly where I am, but this part of the island isn't detailed on the map in the same way the rest of it is. Shit.

How the hell do I get back? I could retrace my steps, but I soon realize I've turned and zigged and zagged all over the place.

Well, this is great. Marvelous. I am lost.

Still, the others know the island well. They will come and find me, I am sure of it.

I can hear the ocean from here, so I decide to take a look, and walk in that direction. Eventually, I'll have to reach the beach.

Hopefully, they won't be too long because I'm more than a little scared right now.

Chapter Nineteen
Wilder

I STARE AT BRODY AND resist the urge to strangle him. He's hiding something. I can tell. You don't spend as much time in the proximity of the same people like we do and not learn when one of them is telling a pack of lies.

"Why would she run off like that?" Rafferty asks.

Good question. Why, indeed? Brody turned up ten minutes ago, out of breath and limping. He said Honor had fled and run toward the cliffs, and the steep drops to the ocean from the part of the island we don't use for any of the hunts.

"You told her to make it primal and to run, so I guess she did," Brody says.

"How about you don't guess, and, instead, you tell us exactly what happened," I say.

"I tripped, and she ran off, probably thinking it was part of the game, but she went in that direction. I shouted at her not to, but I don't think she heard me."

"What the fuck did you do to her?" Asher snarls as he gets right up in Brody's face.

"I didn't do anything, you fucker. I treated her the way we are all supposed to be, like our toy, like a thing. I got her on her knees and made her crawl, and then I fell, and she ran."

"You're not supposed to play alone. It's in the new contract." Rafferty shakes his head.

"Oh, and I suppose the secret safeword you and she have, that's okay, though, right?" Brody snorts out an angry breath. "She's fucking coming between us and messing it all up."

"Is it true that you have a secret safeword?" Asher demands.

"It's needed," Rafferty says.

Jesus fucking Christ, since when did we all start acting independently?

"You should have told us," I say.

"There was nothing duplicitous in it. I thought you'd all enjoy the games more if you had the fantasy it was real, but come on, you had to know I'd legally cover our backs. Deep down."

I pinch the bridge of my nose. Then I turn on my heel and head into the resort.

"Where are you going?" Rafferty snaps.

"To get some supplies and go track Honor. We need to find her before nightfall. The temperature is due to drop this afternoon, and by late evening it will be cold. She's not dressed for it. Rain is forecast for later, and that means she will be wet and cold, and there's no shelter on the side of the island where she is."

"It's not the Arctic." Brody laughs. "She'll survive."

I scowl at him. How can he not care? "You know how easy a person can get hypothermic. She's going to be hot and sweaty right now. As it clouds over later and the breeze gets up, the temperature will drop, and she will get cold quick. Add in rain later, and she could get cold enough to be in trouble. Yeah, she's not likely to die, but she's going to be miserable, and freezing, and perhaps get sick. I'd rather find her before that happens."

Rafferty follows me. "We can check the cameras. We might spot her on one of them."

"I'll do that," Asher volunteers.

I sense us coming together again, united in our mission to find Snow. Only Brody is left out, and, from his expression, I can tell this isn't panning out the way he'd thought.

I pause for a moment. "We need you, too, Brody. You're the one who saw her last. You know exactly what spot she ran from and which direction she went."

Other than me, he's also the one who does best in a survival situation.

A part of me wants to grab the front of his shirt and get up in his face, but it won't help. I'm starting to understand what Brody's problem is, his words ringing in my ears.

She's coming between us, and messing it all up...

So, that's what's got Brody all fucked up. He's worried Honor is going to divide us. The ironic thing is that right now, she's bringing us back together again. He just can't see it. If only he'd let his guard down and embrace her the way the rest of us have, he'd see she's not a threat to us.

Right now, though, I can't deal with Brody's insecurities. Honor is somewhere on the island, and I need to find her. The thought of her lost and frightened does something strange to my insides. I have the sole purpose of locating her pushing at my back, and I won't let anything distract me.

What if she dies? What if she falls from a cliff or tries to swim back around and drowns? I torture myself with finding her limp, lifeless body and have to stifle a roar of rage and grief. If that happens, will we blame Brody? Maybe he's right. Even in death, she'd come between us.

I force the thought from my head. I can't think that way. Honor will be fine, and she can tell us exactly what happened, and then we'll deal with Brody. We need to do something that goes completely against our normal instincts and just sit down and talk it all out. I'm sure once Brody understands that we can make this work with Honor, he'll change his mind. I just hope she'll feel the same way and won't decide to leave. I won't blame her if she does, but deep down, I think she's as addicted to us as we are to her.

I reach the supply closest and dive inside, automatically putting my hands on exactly what I need. I take a pad of paper and pen to record notes and observations as I'm tracking her. Keeping a record of distances and directions, of angles of footprints or broken vegetation will all help me to find her. I'll use the camera on my phone to record things, too. The weather looks as though it's going to be against us, but there's nothing I can do about that.

I rejoin Brody. "Come on. You need to show me the exact spot you last saw her."

I could probably work it out for myself, but it'll be quicker this way.

Brody stares at me for a moment, his lips tight, and then he nods and sets off. I'm right on his heels. His ankle is clearly still bothering him—I can tell by the way he favors his other leg—but he doesn't complain.

It takes us a short hike across the island, but then Brody comes to a stop.

"Here," he says. "That's the rock I tripped on."

"And which direction did she go in?"

He points west.

I hesitate. Do I want to bring Brody with me? I'm unsure. If he frightened her, she might not want to see him. I don't want her to run again if she sees him with me.

"Thanks," I say. "You can go back to the resort now, help the others check the cameras."

There are a lot of them, and they cover the whole island.

He shakes his head. "You're trying to get rid of me. Why? So you can have Honor all to yourself?"

"Jesus, man," I say. "I just want to find her."

"Bros before hoes," he says. "Since when did she come first?"

I bristle. "Don't call her that."

"Isn't that what she is? What all of them are?"

"Firstly, no, they aren't whores. They are women who enjoy the same things we do or are willing to do it for the money. The same way you fought and killed for money." I shouldn't say it, but he's pissing me off. "As for Honor. She's different, and you know it. That's what's got you all freaked out."

He scowls. "I'm not wrong, though, am I? That's the whole point. That's why she needs to leave."

"You sound like you're fucking jealous, man. Jealous of a girl. Are you worried we're going to love her more than we love you?"

"Isn't that exactly what's happening?"

I pause, considering my words. "No one will ever be more important than the four of us, got it? But there is no reason the four of us can't become five, if everyone is agreed."

He does a double take. "Jesus fucking Christ. Since when did this turn into what you're proposing? At least you're saying the quiet part out loud. I knew you were the worst of the bunch of us when it comes to her. Plotting to make her part of us. It won't fucking work."

"Why not?" I shake my head.

"She's *not like us*. She hasn't been through what we have."

"No, but she's been through shit of her own. I don't know what her stepfather did to her, but I'm pretty sure there was at least the promise of abuse there."

"You don't know shit."

"Why else would she be hiding out here with us four, fuckhead?"

He knows I have a point.

I exhale. "I don't have time for this right now, Brody, okay? I need to find her. Once we know she's safe, we'll talk. All five of us. Out in the open, souls laid bare, that kind of thing. We'll figure this out."

I don't wait for his response. I put my head down and move at a slow trot in the direction Brody had pointed out. I make sure I don't move too quickly, not wanting to miss anything.

I know Honor, and I have that advantage. I know her exact size and shape and weight off by heart. I can picture her perfectly in my mind. I know what she's carrying and what she is wearing and what shoe size she has on. I know she's an optimist, despite everything we've put her through, and that she's determined. Knowing these things about her means

I expect her to keep going, believing she can walk her way out of her situation, rather than giving up and huddling down somewhere.

She won't be deliberately doing anything to hide her tracks—or at least, I hope she won't—but I guess that depends on how much she's worried about Brody following her.

I keep my eyes on the ground, looking for any sign that Honor has been this way. The obvious signs are footprints, but they're not always easy to come across, especially if the ground is hard, like it is on the rockier parts of the island. That the weather has been hot lately also makes for a hard ground. There are other things I can make note of, however. If Honor is frightened and running, there may be scatter where soil and other debris is thrown out of track from where she's kicked the ground or soil has stuck to her shoe. I can also watch out for overturned rocks, where the bottom is now showing darker and damp from the ground. If she's come through this way recently, I might also spot disturbed grass and bent blades, which will tell me the direction of her travel. Broken spiderwebs and branches can also indicate that she's come through this way.

There's one other thing I'm watching out for, too, though I haven't dared mention it to the others, and that's blood.

I didn't see any sign of it on Brody, and if he'd hurt her, I was sure I'd see some spatter or marks on his hands, but that doesn't mean she isn't injured. I want to believe my friend isn't capable of hurting her, but Brody suffers from PTSD. Something might have happened where he'd believed himself to be back in the war and she was the enemy. I liked to think he would have mentioned it to me if something like that had happened, but I could be wrong.

All I know is that every minute counts.

I have to find her.

Chapter Twenty
Honor

MY LEGS ACHE, AND MY arms are covered in scratches from brambles. I told myself that as long as I keep the ocean to my left, I'll make it back to the beach, but the topography and vegetation of the island keep blocking my path and pushing me inland.

My backpack is lighter now. I've finished my water and eaten the snack bars. I'd considered making them last, but I'd once read that when in a survival situation, trying to make things last wasn't the best plan. It was better to be fully hydrated and energized to make smart decisions early on, than tired and dehydrated so your brain and body don't work properly.

This isn't a real survival situation, though, I keep telling myself, trying to push down the creeping wave of panic inside me. It's not as though I can walk and walk forever. At some point, I'm going to find the resort, or the guys will find me. Didn't they say there are cameras all over this place? I've been keeping an eye out for the cameras in the trees or boulders, if only so I can stop and wave my arms and jump up and down in the hope of getting noticed, but I haven't seen any. They must be really well hidden.

The rain that's started isn't helping either. It's more of a fine mist than a full rain, but it's come off the sea and is ice-cold, settling on my skin and sinking into my clothes. By the time I remembered the waterproof jacket in my bag, I was already wet through, plus I'd already been damp from sweat. Now I'm a strange combination of hot and chilled, almost feverish, and my energy is leaving me by the minute.

Fucking Brody. Why does he have to be such a dick at times? I don't want to hate him, but he's making it very difficult for me to like him right now. I wonder what he's said to the others and what they'll think in return. I'm sure he won't tell them the whole truth. I'm torn about it, though. If I tell the others what Brody said and did, it'll only widen the divide between us. From what Brody said, I think it's exactly that divide that he's worried about. It explains why he's been so hostile toward me. He thinks I'm going to come between him and the others, and if I go back to the resort and tell them what happened, that's exactly what I'll be doing.

If I don't say anything, will it show Brody he can trust me? Or will it make him think he can get away with doing whatever he wants to me?

One thing I know for sure, I won't be quitting.

Brody won't get what he wants.

Ahead, I catch a glimpse of white through the trees, and my heart lurches. It's definitely something manmade, though I don't think I'm anywhere near the resort. I keep going, pushing my way through the undergrowth, ignoring the brambles that snatch at my face.

What I've found takes shape, and I laugh in delight and relief.

I've reached a cove, and there, bobbing not too far out from shore, is a small white boat. Thank God. It must be one of the boats the guys keep around the island so that whoever is playing their games doesn't need to then hike back across once they've been caught. I've already experienced this service for myself.

There's movement on deck, and a man steps out. He catches sight of me and lifts his hand in a wave. He looks Hispanic. It must be one of the resort workers. He's still at too great a distance for me to make out his features in any detail, but I'm sure the guys will have noticed me missing by now and will have scrambled everyone who works for them to find me.

I'm cold and wet, and just delighted to see another human again.

I return the wave and pick up my pace, scrambling down some rocks to reach the narrow cove. My boots sink into the sand. Soon, I'll be back in the resort, and I can soak in a hot bath and get a change of clothes and have a good meal brought to me. I've long since eaten the energy bars that were in my backpack, and the number of miles I've covered has probably burned thousands of calories. My feet are blistered and my legs aching, and I'm covered in scratches and mosquito bites. The only reason I'm not dying of thirst is because of the rain, and though I'm shivering with the cold, I'm fully aware that my situation would have been a hell of a lot worse if it were sunny. I'd have run out of water a lot sooner, and though I'm not an expert, I'm pretty sure sunstroke and dehydration would be far more dangerous than catching a chill.

The boat is large enough to have a cabin, so it can't get right up to shore. I wonder if I'm going to have to swim to get to it, but then the man onboard unhooks a small dingy attached to the side of the boat and lowers it into the water. He clambers in after it and uses two oars to row ashore.

I'm already wet from the rain, so I wade in to meet him. Waves lap around my ankles and then my shins, but I don't care. The dingy gets closer and closer, until I'm able to make eye contact with the man rowing. I still don't recognize him, but it doesn't matter.

When he's close enough to hear me, I call out. "Oh, my God. I'm so happy you've found me. Thank you so much."

He offers me a warm smile. "You're welcome, miss. I'm happy to have found you, too."

He puts out a hand to help me aboard the small dingy. I slip my palm into his, and he hauls me onboard. I'm not very graceful about it, half-climbing, half-tumbling in, but I can laugh at myself now.

For a minute there, I'd been genuinely worried I wasn't going to be found. I didn't want to spend a night outside, especially not wet and with the temperature dropping.

I shiver and rub my hands up my arms. My rescuer notices.

"Get inside the cabin and warm up."

"I will, thank you. I'm sorry, I didn't catch your name."

"Edwardo," he tells me.

"Thank you again, Edwardo. I'd gotten a bit out of my depth there."

We reach the boat, and he attaches a rope to the side of it, beside a small ladder, and helps me climb onto it. The rise and fall of the ocean beneath me makes me cling even tighter to the metal rungs, but I force myself to let go of one hand at a time so I can climb. Edwardo follows me up, and soon we're both standing on deck.

I let out a sigh of relief.

"Thank you again. How long will it take us to get back to the resort?"

From the cabin, a different male voice sends ice through my veins. It's a voice that's chased me through my nightmares. One I'd hoped to never hear again.

"Oh, you're not going back to the resort."

Chapter Twenty-One
Rafferty

"SHE'S NOT ON THE ISLAND."

I stare at Wilder. "What the fuck are you talking about? Of course she is. Where else would she be?"

"She's not on the fucking island. I'm telling you this for a fact."

He's a big man, and he's pacing and pulling at his long hair. He looks like he's about to explode.

"You must have missed her."

He spins around and slams his fist into a wall. Plasterboard bursts inward, like a bomb has detonated.

"Listen to what I'm fucking telling you, Rafferty. I've tracked her across the island. She went down to a cove, and then her prints stop. So, either she decided to take a fucking long swim, or she got on a boat."

Cold dread settles inside me. "A boat."

He stares at me. "A boat," he confirms. "I think someone's taken her."

Behind Wilder, Asher launches himself at Brody, swinging for him. But Brody is bigger and military trained, and he ducks out of Asher's way and throws a punch instead. It catches Asher in the gut, doubling him over.

"Enough," I roar. "Stop it, both of you. This isn't going to help anyone."

Asher points at Brody. "This is his fault. He lost her."

"I didn't fucking lose her. She ran! Isn't that what this whole game is supposed to be about? Her running and us catching her. It's not my fault if we fucked up the catching her part."

I need to take control of this situation. I don't want the others to see how panicked I feel right now.

"Asher, what about the cameras? Did we spot anyone on the island who shouldn't be?"

He eyes me intensely. "What are you thinking?"

"Someone like her stepfather?"

"The rain has made it hard to see anything," Asher says. "But how would he even know where she is?"

He checks the cameras and then scratches at his jaw as he checks again. "Two of them are out. Near the far cove."

"And you didn't think to say?" Wilder demands.

"I've only just fucking noticed. We have hundreds of them, and it's dark out there and raining."

Shit, this is not good. I doubt two cameras at the same location are out by accident. I turn to Asher and ensure I modulate my tone.

"When you were doing a search on her the other day, did you ever use her real name?"

He frowns, suddenly flustered, in a way he normally isn't. "Yeah, well, of course. How else would have found out about her?"

"And did you disguise your location then?"

He pales. "I didn't think I needed to. We are pretty heavily armed here, and we aren't the kind of men to be messed with."

I rake my hand into my hair. "Fuck. That must be how he found her. He had some kind of alert set up for when someone searched her name. You led him straight to us."

"I was careful!" Asher blurts. "When I let her speak to her friend the other day, I made sure I masked the location."

"You let her speak to her friend?" I say in disbelief. "Jesus, Asher. I thought you were the smart one."

"The girl made him dumb," Brody comments.

We all glare at him.

I shake my head. "It doesn't matter. It was too late by that point, anyway."

Wilder stops pacing. "What the fuck are we going to do?"

I harden my jaw. "We're going to find her. Nothing else matters now, got it? Not dumb-fuck arguments between ourselves. Not even revenge on Wren, not right at this moment. Once we find her and we know she's safe, we can plan two revenges. Wren and whoever took Honor."

I look around at the men, lingering on Brody the longest. "Are we agreed?"

They all give me a nod, even Brody.

"Yeah," he says softly. "Agreed."

"Can we admit she's not going anywhere?" Asher asks. "And work out the fucking difficulties that might cause like adults?" He side-eyes Brody.

"When we get her back, I'll tie her to her fucking bed forever if that is what it takes to keep her safe," Wilder snarls.

"Okay, we are agreed." I look at them all.

"We're going to find our girl, and we're going to bring her home."

About the Authors:
Skye Jones

Redeeming dark and dangerous heroes one book at a time.

Skye Jones is an award winning and USA Today Bestselling Author.

She writes dark mafia and contemporary romance as SR Jones, and angsty paranormal romance as Skye.

When not writing Skye can be found reading, dog herding, or watching gritty dramas on Netflix with her husband. She lives in the grey, windswept north of England, which fuels her taste for the dramatic and the gothic.

For a free read sign up for her reader club here: https://dl.bookfunnel.com/ca20ewxx71

About the Authors:
Marissa Farrar

Marissa Farrar has always been in love with being in love. But since she's been married for numerous years and has three young daughters, she's conducted her love affairs with multiple gorgeous men of the fictional persuasion.

The author of more than thirty novels, she has been a full time author for the last six years. She predominantly writes paranormal romance and fantasy, but has branched into contemporary fiction as well.

To stay updated on all her new Reverse Harem books, just sign up to her newsletter and grab a free short story from her Dark Codes series. https://dl.bookfunnel.com/4t79xdwx8m

You can also find her at her facebook page, www.facebook.com/marissa.farrar.author

Or join her facebook group, https://www.facebook.com/groups/1336965479667766

She loves to hear from readers and can be emailed at marissafarrar@hotmail.co.uk.

Printed in Great Britain
by Amazon